PRESENCE

PRESENCE

Stories

Arthur Miller

VIKING

VIKING

Published by the Penguin Group

Penguin Group (USA) Inc., 375 Hudson Street,
New York, New York 10014, U.S.A.
Penguin Group (Canada), 90 Eglinton Avenue East, Suite 700, Toronto,
Ontario, Canada M4P 2Y3 (a division of Pearson Penguin Canada Inc.)
Penguin Books Ltd, 80 Strand, London WC2R 0RL, England
Penguin Ireland, 25 St. Stephen's Green, Dublin 2, Ireland (a division of Penguin Books Ltd)
Penguin Books Australia Ltd, 250 Camberwell Road, Camberwell,
Victoria 3124, Australia (a division of Pearson Australia Group Pty Ltd)
Penguin Books India Pvt Ltd, 11 Community Centre,
Panchsheel Park, New Delhi –110 017, India
Penguin Group (NZ), 67 Apollo Drive, Mairangi Bay, Auckland 1311,
New Zealand (a division of Pearson New Zealand Ltd.)
Penguin Books (South Africa) (Pty) Ltd, 24 Sturdee Avenue,
Rosebank, Johannesburg 2196, South Africa

Penguin Books Ltd, Registered Offices: 80 Strand, London WC2R 0RL, England

First published in 2007 by Viking Penguin, a member of Penguin Group (USA) Inc.

1 3 5 7 9 10 8 6 4 2

"Bulldog," "The Performance," and "The Bare Manuscript" first appeared in *The New Yorker;*
"Beavers" in *Harper's*; "The Turpentine Still" in *Southwest Review*; and "Presence" in *Esquire.*

ISBN: 978-0-670-03828-2

Printed in the United States of America
Set in Celeste · Designed by Francesca Belanger

Contents

PRESENCE

BULLDOG

He saw this tiny ad in the paper: "Black Brindle Bull puppies, $3.00 each." He had something like ten dollars from his housepainting job, which he hadn't deposited yet, but they had never had a dog in the house. His father was taking a long nap when the idea crested in his mind, and his mother, in the middle of a bridge game when he asked her if it would be all right, shrugged absently and threw a card. He walked around the house trying to decide, and the feeling spread through him that he'd better hurry, before somebody else got the puppy first. In his mind, there was already one particular puppy that belonged to him—it was his puppy and the puppy knew it. He had no idea what a brindle bull looked like, but it sounded tough and wonderful. And he had the three dollars, though it soured him to think of spending it when they had such bad money worries, with his father gone bankrupt again. The tiny ad hadn't mentioned how many puppies there were. Maybe there were only two or three, which might be bought by this time.

The address was on Schermerhorn Street, which he had never heard of. He called, and a woman with a husky voice explained how to get there and on which line. He was coming from the Midwood section, and the elevated Culver line, so he would have to change at Church Avenue. He wrote everything down and read it all back to her. She still had the puppies, thank God. It took more than an hour, but the train was almost empty, this being Sunday, and with a breeze from its open wood-framed windows it was cooler than down in the street. Below in empty lots he could see old Italian women, their heads covered with red bandannas, bent over and loading their aprons with dandelions. His Italian school friends said they were for wine and salads. He remembered trying to eat one once when he was playing left field in the lot near his house, but it was bitter and salty as tears. The old wooden train, practically unloaded, rocked and clattered lightly through the hot afternoon. He passed above a block where men were standing in driveways watering their cars as though they were hot elephants. Dust floated pleasantly through the air.

The Schermerhorn Street neighborhood was a surprise, totally different from his own, in Midwood. The houses here were made of brownstone, and were not at all like the clapboard ones on his block, which had been put up only a few years before or, in the earliest cases, in the twenties. Even the sidewalks looked old, with big squares of stone instead of cement, and bits of grass growing in the cracks between them. He could tell that Jews didn't live here, maybe because it was so quiet and unenergetic and not a soul was sitting outside to enjoy the sun. Lots of windows were wide open, with expressionless people leaning on their elbows and staring out, and cats stretched out on some of the sills, many of the women in their bras and the men in underwear trying to catch a breeze. Trickles of sweat were creeping down his back, not only from the heat but also because he realized now that he was the only one who wanted the dog, since his parents hadn't really had an opinion and his brother, who was older, had said, "What are you, crazy, spending your few dollars on a puppy? Who knows if it will be any good? And what are you going to feed it?" He thought bones, and his brother, who always knew what was right or wrong, yelled, "Bones! They have no teeth yet!" Well, maybe soup, he had mumbled. "Soup! You going to feed a puppy *soup*?" Suddenly he saw that he had arrived at the address. Standing there, he felt the bottom falling out, and he knew it was all a mistake, like one of his dreams or a lie that he had stupidly tried to defend as being real. His heart sped up and he felt he was blushing and walked on for half a block or so. He was the only one out, and people in a few of the windows were watching him on the empty street. But how could he go home after he had come so far? It seemed he'd been travelling for weeks or a year. And now to get back on the subway with nothing? Maybe he ought at least to get a look at the puppy, if the woman would let him. He had looked it up in the Book of Knowledge, where they had two full pages of dog pictures, and there had been a white English bulldog with bent front legs and teeth that stuck out from its lower jaw, and a little black-and-white Boston bull, and a long-nosed pit bull, but they had no picture of a brindle bull. When you came down to it, all he really knew about brindle bulls was that they would cost three dollars. But he had to at least get a look at him, his puppy, so he went back down the block and rang the basement doorbell, as the woman had told him to do. The sound was so loud it startled him, but he felt if he ran away and she came out in time to see him it would be even more embarrassing, so he stood there with sweat running down over his lip.

An inner door under the stoop opened, and a woman came out and looked at him through the dusty iron bars of the gate. She wore some kind of gown, light-pink silk, which she held together with one hand, and she had long black hair down to her shoulders. He didn't dare look directly into her face, so he couldn't tell exactly what she looked like, but he could feel her tension as she stood there behind her closed gate. He felt she could not imagine what he was doing ringing her bell and he quickly asked if she was the one who'd put the ad in. Oh! Her manner changed right away, and she unlatched the gate and pulled it open. She was shorter than he and had a peculiar smell, like a mixture of milk and stale air. He followed her into the apartment, which was so dark he could hardly make out anything, but he could hear the high yapping of puppies. She had to yell to ask him where he lived and how old he was, and when he told her thirteen she clapped a hand over her mouth and said that he was very tall for his age, but he couldn't understand why this seemed to embarrass her, except that she may have thought he was fifteen, which people sometimes did. But even so. He followed her into the kitchen, at the back of the apartment, where finally he could see around him, now that he'd been out of the sun for a few minutes. In a large cardboard box that had been unevenly cut down to make it shallower he saw three puppies and their mother, who sat looking up at him with her tail moving slowly back and forth. He didn't think she looked like a bulldog, but he didn't dare say so. She was just a brown dog with flecks of black and a few stripes here and there, and the puppies were the same. He did like the way their little ears drooped, but he said to the woman that he had wanted to see the puppies but hadn't made up his mind yet. He really didn't know what to do next, so, in order not to seem as though he didn't appreciate the puppies, he asked if she would mind if he held one. She said that was all right and reached down into the box and lifted out two puppies and set them down on the blue linoleum. They didn't look like any bulldogs he had ever seen, but he was embarrassed to tell her that he didn't really want one. She picked one up and said, "Here," and put it on his lap.

He had never held a dog before and was afraid it would slide off, so he cradled it in his arms. It was hot on his skin and very soft and kind of disgusting in a thrilling way. It had gray eyes like tiny buttons. It troubled him that the Book of Knowledge hadn't had a picture of this kind of dog. A real bulldog was kind of tough and dangerous, but these were just brown dogs. He sat there on the arm of the green upholstered chair with the puppy on his lap, not knowing what to do next. The woman, meanwhile, had put herself next to him, and it felt like she had given his hair a pat, but he wasn't sure because he had very thick hair. The more seconds that ticked away the less sure he was of what to do. Then she asked if he would like some water, and he said he would, and she went to the faucet and ran water, which gave him a chance to stand up and set the puppy back in the box. She came back to him holding the glass and as he took it she let her gown fall open, showing her breasts like half-filled balloons, saying she couldn't believe he was only thirteen. He gulped the water and started to hand her back the glass, and she suddenly drew his head to her and kissed him. In all this time, for some reason, he hadn't been able to look into her face, and when he tried to now he couldn't see anything but a blur and hair. She reached down to him and a shivering started in the backs of his legs. It got sharper, until it was almost like the time he touched the live rim of a light socket while trying to remove a broken bulb. He would never be able to remember getting down on the carpet—he felt like a waterfall was smashing down on top of his head. He remembered getting inside her heat and his head banging and banging against the leg of her couch. He was almost at Church Avenue, where he had to change for the elevated Culver line, before realizing she hadn't taken his three dollars, and he couldn't recall agreeing to it but he had this small cardboard box on his lap with a puppy mewling inside. The scraping of nails on the cardboard sent chills up his back. The woman, as he remembered now, had cut two holes into the top of the box, and the puppy kept sticking his nose through them.

His mother jumped back when he untied the cord and the puppy pushed up and scrambled out, yapping. "What is he doing?" she yelled, with her hands in the air as though she were about to be attacked. By this time, he'd lost his fear of the puppy and held him in his arms and let him lick his face, and seeing this his mother calmed down a bit. "Is he hungry?" she asked, and stood with her mouth slightly open, ready for anything, as he put the puppy on the floor again. He said the puppy might be hungry, but he thought he could eat only soft things, although his little teeth were as sharp as pins. She got out some soft cream cheese and put a little piece of it on the floor, but the

puppy only sniffed at it and peed. "My God in Heaven!" she
yelled, and quickly got a piece of newspaper to blot it up with.
When she bent over that way, he thought of the woman's heat
and was ashamed and shook his head. Suddenly her name
came to him—Lucille—which she had told him when they
were on the floor. Just as he was slipping in, she had opened
her eyes and said, "My name is Lucille." His mother brought
out a bowl of last night's noodles and set it on the floor. The
puppy raised his little paw and tipped the bowl over, spilling
some of the chicken soup at the bottom. This he began to lick
hungrily off the linoleum. "He likes chicken soup!" his mother
yelled happily, and immediately decided he would most likely
enjoy an egg and so put water on to boil. Somehow the puppy
knew that she was the one to follow and walked behind her,
back and forth, from the stove to the refrigerator. "He follows
me!" his mother said, laughing happily.

On his way home from school the next day, he stopped at the
hardware store and bought a puppy collar for seventy-five
cents, and Mr. Schweckert threw in a piece of clothesline as a
leash. Every night as he fell asleep, he brought out Lucille like
something from a secret treasure box and wondered if he could
dare phone her and maybe be with her again. The puppy, which
he had named Rover, seemed to grow noticeably bigger every
day, although he still showed no signs of looking like any bulldog. The boy's father thought Rover should live in the cellar,
but it was very lonely down there and he would never stop yapping. "He misses his mother," his mother said, so every night
the boy started him off on some rags in an old wash basket

down there, and when he'd yapped enough the boy was allowed to bring him up and let him sleep on some rags in the
kitchen, and everybody was thankful for the quiet. His mother
tried to walk the puppy in the quiet street they lived on, but he
kept tangling the rope around her ankles, and because she was
afraid to hurt him she exhausted herself following him in all
his zigzags. It didn't always happen, but many times when the
boy looked at Rover he'd think of Lucille and could almost feel
the heat again. He would sit on the porch steps stroking the
puppy and think of her, the insides of her thighs. He still couldn't
imagine her face, just her long black hair and her strong neck.

One day, his mother baked a chocolate cake and set it to
cool on the kitchen table. It was at least eight inches thick, and
he knew it would be delicious. He was drawing a lot in those
days, pictures of spoons and forks or cigarette packages or, occasionally, his mother's Chinese vase with the dragon on it,
anything that had an interesting shape. So he put the cake on a
chair next to the table and drew for a while and then got up and
went outside for some reason and got involved with the tulips
he had planted the previous fall that were just now showing
their tips. Then he decided to go look for a practically new baseball he had mislaid the previous summer and which he was
sure, or pretty sure, must be down in the cellar in a cardboard
box. He had never really got down to the bottom of that box,
because he was always distracted by finding something he'd
forgotten he had put in there. He had started down into the
cellar from the outside entrance, under the back porch, when
he noticed that the pear tree, which he had planted two years
before, had what looked like a blossom on one of its slender

branches. It amazed him, and he felt proud and successful. He had paid thirty-five cents for the tree on Court Street and thirty cents for an apple tree, which he planted about seven feet away, so as to be able to hang a hammock between them someday. They were still too thin and young, but maybe next year. He always loved to stare at the two trees, because he had planted them, and he felt they somehow knew he was looking at them, and even that they were looking back at him. The back yard ended at a ten-foot-high wooden fence that surrounded Erasmus Field, where the semi-pro and sandlot teams played on weekends, teams like the House of David and the Black Yankees and the one with Satchel Paige, who was famous as one of the country's greatest pitchers except he was a Negro and couldn't play in the big leagues, obviously. The House of Davids all had long beards—he'd never understood why, but maybe they were Orthodox Jews, although they didn't look it. An extremely long foul shot over right field could drop a ball into the yard, and that was the ball it had occurred to him to search for, now that spring had come and the weather was warming up. In the basement, he found the box and was immediately surprised at how sharp his ice skates were, and recalled that he had once had a vise to clamp the skates side by side so that a stone could be rubbed on the blades. He pushed aside a torn fielder's glove, a hockey goalie's glove whose mate he knew had been lost, some pencil stubs and a package of crayons, and a little wooden man whose arms flapped up and down when you pulled a string. Then he heard the puppy yapping over his head, but it was not his usual sound—it was continuous and very sharp and loud. He ran upstairs and saw his mother coming down into the living

room from the second floor, her dressing gown flying out behind her, a look of fear on her face. He could hear the scraping
of the puppy's nails on the linoleum, and he rushed into the
kitchen. The puppy was running around and around in a circle
and sort of screaming, and the boy could see at once that his
belly was swollen. The cake was on the floor, and most of it was
gone. "My cake!" his mother screamed, and picked up the dish
with the remains on it and held it up high as though to save it
from the puppy, even though practically nothing was left. The
boy tried to catch Rover, but he slipped away into the living
room. His mother was behind him yelling "The carpet!" Rover
kept running, in wider circles now that he had more space, and
foam was forming on his muzzle. "Call the police!" his mother
yelled. Suddenly, the puppy fell and lay on his side, gasping
and making little squeaks with each breath. Since they had
never had a dog and knew nothing about veterinarians, he
looked in the phone book and found the A.S.P.C.A. number and
called them. Now he was afraid to touch Rover, because the
puppy snapped at his hand when it got close and he had this
foam on his mouth. When the van drew up in front of the
house, the boy went outside and saw a young guy removing a
little cage from the back. He told him that the dog had eaten
practically a whole cake, but the man had no interest and came
into the house and stood for a moment looking down at Rover,
who was making little yips now but was still down on his side.
The man dropped some netting over him and when he slipped
him into the cage, the puppy tried to get up and run. "What do
you think is the matter with him?" his mother asked, her mouth
turned down in revulsion, which the boy now felt in himself.

"What's the matter with him is he ate a cake," the man said. Then he carried the cage out and slid it through the back door into the darkness of the van. "What will you do with him?" the boy asked. "You want him?" the man snapped. His mother was standing on the stoop now and overheard them. "We can't have him here," she called over, with fright and definiteness in her voice, and approached the young man. "We don't know how to keep a dog. Maybe somebody who knows how to keep him would want him." The young man nodded with no interest either way, got behind the wheel, and drove off.

The boy and his mother watched the van until it disappeared around the corner. Inside, the house was dead quiet again. He didn't have to worry anymore about Rover doing something on the carpets or chewing the furniture, or whether he had water or needed to eat. Rover had been the first thing he'd looked for on returning from school every day and on waking in the morning, and he had always worried that the dog might have done something to displease his mother or father. Now all that anxiety was gone and, with it, the pleasure, and it was silent in the house.

He went back to the kitchen table and tried to think of something he could draw. A newspaper lay on one of the chairs, and he opened it and inside saw a Saks stocking ad showing a woman with a gown pulled aside to display her leg. He started copying it and thought of Lucille again. Could he possibly call her, he wondered, and do what they had done again? Except that she would surely ask about Rover, and he couldn't do anything but lie to her. He remembered how she had cuddled Rover in her arms and even kissed his nose. She had really loved that puppy. How could he tell her he was gone? Just sitting and thinking of her he was hardening up like a broom handle and he suddenly thought what if he called her and said his family were thinking of having a second puppy to keep Rover company? But then he would have to pretend he still had Rover, which would mean two lies, and that was a little frightening. Not the lies so much as trying to remember, first, that he still had Rover, second, that he was serious about a second puppy, and, third, the worst thing, that when he got up off Lucille he would have to say that unfortunately he couldn't actually take another puppy because . . . Why? The thought of all that lying exhausted him. Then he visualized being in her heat again and he thought his head would explode, and the idea came that when it was over she might insist on his taking another puppy. Force it on him. After all, she had not accepted his three dollars and Rover had been a sort of gift, he thought. It would be embarrassing to refuse another puppy, especially when he had supposedly come back to her for exactly that reason. He didn't dare go through all that and gave up the whole idea. But then the thought crept back again of her spreading apart on the floor the way she had, and he returned to searching for some reason he could give for not taking another puppy after he had supposedly come all the way across Brooklyn to get one. He could just see the look on her face on his turning down a puppy, the puzzlement or, worse, anger. Yes, she could very possibly get angry and see through him, realizing that all he had come for was to get into her and the rest of it was nonsense, and she might feel insulted. Maybe even slap him. What would he do then? He couldn't fight a grown woman. Then

again, it now occurred to him that by this time she might well
have sold the other two puppies, which at three dollars were
pretty inexpensive. Then what? He began to wonder, suppose
he just called her up and said he'd like to come over again and
see her, without mentioning any puppies? He would have to
tell only one lie, that he still had Rover and that the family all
loved him and so on. He could easily remember that much. He
went to the piano and played some chords, mostly in the dark
bass, to calm himself. He didn't really know how to play, but
he loved inventing chords and letting the vibrations shoot up
his arms. He played, feeling as though something inside him
had sort of shaken loose or collapsed altogether. He was different than he had ever been, not empty and clear anymore but
weighted with secrets and his lies, some told and some untold,
but all of it disgusting enough to set him slightly outside his
family, in a place where he could watch them now, and watch
himself with them. He tried to invent a melody with the right
hand and find matching chords with the left. By sheer luck, he
was hitting some beauties. It was really amazing how his chords
were just slightly off, with a discordant edge but still in some
way talking to the right-hand melody. His mother came into
the room full of surprise and pleasure. "What's happening?"
she called out in delight. She could play and sight-read music
and had tried and failed to teach him, because, she believed, his
ear was too good and he'd rather play what he heard than do
the labor of reading notes. She came over to the piano and stood
beside him, watching his hands. Amazed, wishing as always
that he could be a genius, she laughed. "Are you making this
up?" she almost yelled, as though they were side by side on a

roller coaster. He could only nod, not daring to speak and maybe lose what he had somehow snatched out of the air, and he laughed with her because he was so completely happy that he had secretly changed, and unsure at the same time that he would ever be able to play like this again.

THE PERFORMANCE

Harold May would have been about thirty-five when I met him. With his blondish hair parted in the exact middle, and his horn-rimmed glasses and remarkably round boyish eyes, he resembled Harold Lloyd, the famous bespectacled movie comic with the surprised look. When I think of May, I see a man with rosy cheeks, in a gray suit with white pinstripes and a red-and-blue striped bow tie—a dancer, slender, snugly built, light on his feet and, like a lot of dancers, wrapped up (mummified, you might say) in his art. So he seemed at first, anyway. I see us in a midtown drugstore, the kind that at that time, the forties, had tables where people could sit around for an unemployed hour with their sodas and sundaes. May was wanting to tell a long and involved story, and I wasn't sure why he was bothering but I gradually caught on that it was to interest me in doing a feature about him. My old friend Ralph Barton (né Berkowitz) brought him to me thinking I might make use of his weird story, even though he knew that I had left journalism by then and was no longer sitting around in drugstores and bars, having become sufficiently known as a writer to be embarrassed by strangers accosting me in restaurants or on the

street. This was probably in the spring, only two years after the
end of the war.

As Harold May told it that afternoon, he had been employed
only fitfully back in the mid-thirties, having built a tap-dance
act that had played the Palace twice. While he almost always
got excited *Variety* notices, he could never really escape the devoted but small audiences in places like Queens, Toledo, Ohio,
and Erie or Tonawanda, New York. "If they know how to fit
things together they tend to like watching tap," he said, and it
pleased him that steelworkers particularly loved the act, as well
as machinists, glassblowers—almost anybody who appreciated
skills. By '36, though, Harold, convinced that his head was
bumping the ceiling of his career, was so depressed that when
an offer came to work in Hungary he snapped it up, although
uncertain where that country might be located. He soon learned
that a so-called vaudeville wheel existed in Budapest, Bucha-
rest, Athens, and half a dozen other East European cities, with
Vienna the big prestige booking that would give him lots of
publicity. Once established, an act could work almost year-
round, returning again and again to the same clubs. "They like
things not to change much," he said. Tap, however, was a real
novelty, a purely American dance unknown in Europe, invented as it had been by Negroes in the South, and a lot of Eu-
ropeans were charmed by what they took to be its amusingly
optimistic American ambience.

Harold worked the wheel, he explained to me over the
white-marble-topped table, for some six or eight months. "The
work was steady, the money was decent, and in some places,
like Bulgaria, we were practically stars. Got to go to dinners in

a couple of castles, with women falling all over us, and great wine. I was as happy as I was ever going to get," he said.

With his little troupe of two men and a woman and himself plus a pickup piano player or, in some places, a small band, he had a mobile and efficient business. Still young and unmarried, with his whole short life concentrated on his legs, his shoes, and persisting dreams of glory, he surprised himself now by enjoying sightseeing in the cities of the wheel and picking up odd bits about European history and art. He had only a high-school diploma from Evander Childs and had never had time to think about much beyond his next gig, so Europe opened his eyes to a past that he had hardly imagined existed.

In Budapest one night, contentedly removing his makeup in his decrepit La Babalu Club dressing room, he was surprised by the appearance in his doorway of a tall, well-dressed gentleman who bowed slightly from the waist and in German-accented English introduced himself and asked deferentially if he could have a few minutes of May's precious time. Harold invited the German to have a seat on a shredded pink satin chair.

The German, about forty-five, had gleaming, beautifully coiffed silver hair and wore a fine, greenish, heavyweight suit and black high-top shoes. His name was Damian Fugler, he said, and he had come in his official capacity as Cultural Attaché of the German Embassy in Budapest. His English, though accented, was flawlessly exact.

"I have had the pleasure of attending three of your performances now," Fugler began in a rolling baritone, "and first of all wish to pay my respects to you as a fine artist." Nobody had ever called Harold an artist.

"Well, thanks," he managed to say. "I appreciate the compliment." I could imagine the inflation he must have felt, this pink-cheeked young guy out of Berea, Ohio, taking praise from this elegant European with his high-top shoes.

"I myself have performed with the Stuttgart Opera, although not as a singer, of course, but a 'spear-carrier,' as we call it. That was quite a time ago, when I was much younger." Fugler permitted himself a forgiving smile at his youthful pranks. "But I will get down to business—I have been authorized to invite you, Mr. May, to perform in Berlin. My department is prepared to pay your transportation costs as well as hotel expenses."

The breathtaking idea of a government—any government—having an interest in tap dancing was, of course, way beyond imagining for Harold, and it took a moment to digest or even to believe.

"Well, I really don't know what to say. Like where do I play, a club or what?"

"It would be in the Kick Club. You must have heard of it?"

Harold had heard of the Kick Club as one of Berlin's classiest. His heart was banging. But his booking experience warned him to circle around the proposal. "And how long an engagement would this be?" he asked.

"Most probably one performance."

"One?"

"We would require only one, but you would be free to arrange more with the management, provided, of course, they wish you to continue. We are prepared to pay you two thousand dollars for the evening, if that would be satisfactory."

Two thousand for one night! This was practically a normal

year's take. Harold's head was spinning. He knew he ought to be asking questions, but which? "And you? Excuse me, but you are what again?"

Fugler removed a beautiful black leather card case from his breast pocket and handed Harold a card, which he tried unsuccessfully to focus on once he glimpsed the sharply embossed eagle clutching a swastika, which flew up like a dart into his brain.

"Could I let you know tomorrow?" he began, but Fugler's mellow baritone voice quickly cut him off.

"I'm afraid you would have to leave sometime tomorrow. I have arranged with the management here to free you from your contract, should you find that agreeable."

Free him from his contract! "I felt," he said to me over his half-empty chocolate-soda glass, "that unbeknownst to me people had been discussing me in some high office somewhere. It was scary, but you can't help feeling important," he said, and laughed like a wicked adolescent.

"May I ask why so soon?" he asked Fugler.

"I'm afraid I am not at liberty to say more than that my superiors will not have the time to see your performance after Thursday, at least not for several weeks or possibly months." Suddenly the man was leaning forward over Harold's knees, his face nearly touching Harold's hand, his voice lowered to a whisper. "This may change your life, Mr. May. You cannot possibly hesitate."

With two grand dangling before him, Harold heard himself saying, "All right." The whole encounter was so weird that he immediately began to backtrack and ask for more time to decide, but the German was gone. In his hand he saw a five-hundred-dollar bill and vaguely recalled the accented baritone voice saying, "As a deposit. Berlin then! *Auf Wiedersehen.*"

"He'd never even offered me a contract," Harold told us, "just left the money."

He barely slept that night, castigating himself. "You like to think you're in charge of yourself, but this Fugler was like a hurricane." What particularly bothered him now, he said, was his having agreed to the single performance. What was that about? "Over the months, I'd gotten used to not bothering to understand what was going on around me—I mean, I didn't know a word of Hungarian, Romanian, Bulgarian, German—but a single performance? I couldn't figure out what it could mean."

And why the big hurry? "I was stumped," he said. "I wished to God I'd never taken the money. At the same time, I couldn't help being curious."

His mind was somewhat eased by the troupe's delight at getting out of the Balkans, and at his sharing some of his advance among them, and on the train north they were jounced with life and this cockeyed adventure. The prospect of playing Berlin—the capital of Europe, second only to Paris—was like going to a party. Harold ordered champagne and steaks and tried to relax among his dancers and smooth out his anxieties. As the train clanked northward, he contrasted his luck with his probable situation had he stayed in New York, with its lines of unemployed and the unbroken grip of the American slump.

When the train stopped at the German border, an officer opened the door of his compartment, which Harold shared with Benny Worth, who had been with him the longest, and two Romanians, who slept almost continuously, but did waken

occasionally, smile briefly, and return to their dreams. The officer, Harold thought, scowled at him as he opened his passport.
He had been scowled at by border guards any number of times
on this tour, but this German's scowl touched something very
deep in his body. It was more than his suddenly remembering
that he was Jewish; he had never really had a problem with being Jewish, especially since his blond hair, blue eyes, and gener-
ally happy nature had never invited the usual reactions of the
era. It was, rather, that until now he had managed to erase almost totally the stories he had read a year or so earlier about
the young German government's having staged rallies against
Jews, driving them out of businesses and professions, closing
synagogues, and forcing many to emigrate. On the other hand,
Benny Worth, who called himself a Communist and had all
kinds of information that never appeared in regular papers like
The New York Times, had told him that the Nazis had been
tamping down on the anti-Jewish stuff this year so as not to
look nasty for the Olympic tourists. In any case, none of this
had applied to him personally. "I'd heard some bad stories of
Romanian incidents, too, but I never saw anything, so I could
never keep them in my head," he explained. I could understand
this; after all, he'd had no verbal contact with his audiences and
could not read local papers, so that a certain remoteness was
wrapped around anything real going on in the cities he had
been playing.

In fact, he said, his one distinct impression of Hitler had
come from a newsreel that showed him walking out of the
Olympics a few months earlier when Jesse Owens, the Negro
runner, mounted the platform to accept his fourth gold medal.

"Which was pretty bad sportsmanship," he said, "but let's face it, something like that could have happened in lots of places." The truth was, Harold had a hard time concentrating on politics at all. His life was tap, nailing his next gig, keeping edible food on his table and his troupe from splitting up and forcing him to train new people in his routines. And, of course, with his American passport in his pocket, he could always pick up and pull out and go back to the Balkans or even home, if worst came to worst.

They arrived in Berlin on Tuesday evening and were met as they stepped down from the train by two men, one in a suit resembling Fugler's but blue instead of green, and the other in a black uniform with white piping down the edges of the lapels. "Mr. Fugler is awaiting you," the uniformed one said, and Harold caught his own importance in this and could hardly control the thrill it gave him; normally he and his troupe emerged from trains hauling their heavy leather luggage while struggling with some idiotic foreign language to direct porters and hail cabs, usually in the rain. Here, they were led into a Mercedes, which gravely proceeded to the Adlon Hotel, the best in Berlin and maybe in all Europe. By the time he was finishing his dinner of oysters, osso buco, potato pancakes, and Riesling alone in his room, Harold had buried his qualms in imaginings of what he might do with his newfound money and he was ready to go to work.

Fugler showed up at breakfast next morning and sat down in his room for a few minutes. They would perform at midnight, he said, and would have the club for rehearsals until eight that evening, when the regular show started. This was a slightly more excited Fugler; "He looked like he'd throw his arms around me any minute," Harold said.

"I was getting along so good with Fugler," Harold said, "that I figured it was time to ask who we were supposed to be dancing for. But he just smiled and said security considerations forbade that kind of information and he hoped I'd understand. Frankly, Benny Worth had mentioned that the Duke of Windsor was in town, so we wondered if maybe it was him, seeing he was pretty snug with Hitler."

Breakfast done, they were driven to the club, where they confronted the six-piece house band, whose only member under fifty was Mohammed the Syrian pianist, a sharp young sport with fantastically long brown fingers covered with rings, who knew some English and translated Harold's remarks to the rest of the band. Relishing his new authority, Mohammed proceeded to take revenge on the other players, all Germans, whom he had been trying for months, unsuccessfully, to bring up to tempo. They knew "Swanee River," so Harold had them try that as an accompaniment, but they were hopelessly slack, so he managed to drive off the violinist and the accordionist as diplomatically as possible and worked with the drum and piano and it was tolerable. Waiters and kitchen help started arriving at noon, and he had an amazed audience standing around polishing silver as he went through the troupe's stuff. To dance before applauding waiters was a new experience, and the troupe began to feel golden. They were served a broiled-trout lunch in the empty room, another first, with wine, freshly baked hard rolls, and chocolate cake with marvellous coffee, and by half past two were sharp on their feet but sleepy. A car brought

them back to the Adlon for a nap. They would have dinner at
the club, free, of course.

Harold for a long time lay motionless in a six-foot marble
tub in his habitual pre-performance hot bath. "The faucets were
gold-plated, the towels were yards long." It was the waiters' un-
precedented near-reverence for him and the troupe that forced
him to suspect that his audience tonight had to be some very
high-level Nazi political people. Hitler? He prayed not. His own
stupidity at having failed to insist on knowing appalled him.
He should have deduced this problem the moment Fugler had
said it was to be a single performance. Once again, what I imagined must have been his lifelong curse of timidity soured Harold's mind. Sliding down the bath until his head was underwater,
he said, he tried to drown but finally decided otherwise. What
if they discovered he was Jewish? The images of persecution,
which he had seen in newspapers earlier this year, marched out
of the locked closet hidden in a recess of his mind. But they
couldn't possibly do something to an *American.* Blessing his
passport, he got out of the tub and, dripping wet, fear in his
belly, he checked that it was still in his jacket pocket. The plush
towel on his skin somehow made it even more absurd that he
should be feeling anxiety rather than happy anticipation as a
command performance neared. Standing at a tall, satin-draped
window, tying his bow tie, he stared down at the busy thor-
oughfare, at this very modern city with nicely dressed people
pausing at store windows, greeting each other, tipping hats,
and waiting for traffic lights to change, and felt the craziness of
his position—he was like a scared cat chased up a tree by some
spectre of danger it had glimpsed which might have been only

an awning snapping in the breeze. "Still, I remembered Benny Worth's saying the Nazis' days were numbered because the workers would soon be knocking them out of office—so all hope wasn't lost."

He decided to gather the troupe in his dressing room. Paul Garner and Benny Worth stood in their tuxedos and Carol Conway in her blazing-red filmy number, all of them a little edgy since there was no precedent for Harold's summoning them before a show. "I'm not guaranteeing this, but I have an idea we are dancing for Mr. Hitler tonight." They nearly swelled with the pleasure of their success. Benny Worth, a born team player, his gravelly voice burgeoning through his cigar smoke, clenched his heavy right fist, flashing a diamond ring with which he had more than once wounded interlopers, and said, "Don't worry about that son of a bitch."

Carol, always a quick weeper, looked at Harold with waters threatening her eyes. "But do they know you're—"

"No," he cut her off. "But we'll get out of here tomorrow and go back to Budapest. I just didn't want you to be thrown off—in case you see him sitting there. Just play it the same as usual, and tomorrow we're back on the train."

A massive chandelier hung over the nightclub's circular stage, a blaze of twinkling lights which irritated Harold, who distrusted anything hanging over his head when he danced. The pink walls had a Moorish motif, the tabletops were grass green. They watched through peepholes from behind the orchestra as, promptly at midnight, Herr Bix, the manager, stopped the band, stood center stage, and apologized to the packed room for interrupting the dance, assured the customers of his gratitude for their having come this evening, and announced that it was his "duty" to request everyone to leave. Since normal closing time was around two, everyone imagined an emergency of some sort, and the use of the word "duty" suggested that this emergency involved the regime, so that with only a murmur of surprise the several hundred patrons gathered up their things and filed out into the street.

Some strolled off, others entered cabs, and the stragglers halted at the curb to watch, awed, as the famous long Mercedes appeared and turned in to the alley next to the club, preceded and followed by three or four black cars filled with men.

Through the peepholes, Harold and the troupe watched, amazed, as twenty or so uniformed officers spread out around the Leader, whose table had been moved to within a dozen feet of the stage. With him sat the enormously fat and easily recognized Göring, and another officer, and Fugler. "In fact, they were almost all enormous men; at least, they looked enormous in their uniforms," Harold said. Waiters were filling all their glasses with water, reminding Harold, also practically a non-drinker, of Hitler's reported vegetarianism. Bix, the Kick manager, who had scurried around backstage, now touched Harold's shoulder. Mohammed, no longer in his usual spineless slope over the keyboard but bolt upright, caught the signal from Bix and, with his ringed fingers and with the drummer backing up with his brush, went into "Tea for Two," and Harold was on. The shape of the number could not have been simpler; Harold soloed soft-shoe, went into the shuffle, then, on the third chorus, Worth and Garner cakewalked in from left and right, and finally Carol, as happy temptress, swooned pliably around the formations that were made and unmade and made again. Within a minute, it was obvious to the astonished Harold as he glanced at Hitler's dreaded face that the man was experiencing some profound kind of wild astonishment. The troupe went into the stomp, shoes drumming the stage floor, and Hitler seemed transfixed now, swept up in the booming rhythms, both clenched fists pressing down on the tabletop, his neck stretched taut, his mouth slightly agape. "I thought we were looking at an orgasm," Harold said. Göring, who "began to look like a big fat baby," was lightly tapping the table with his palm and occasionally laughing delightedly in his condescending fashion. And, of course, their retinue, cued by their superiors' clear approval of the performers, was unleashed, ho-ho-ing in competition over who would show the most unmitigated enjoyment. Harold, helplessly enjoying his own triumph, was flying off the tips of his shoes. After so much trepidation, this surprising flow of brutal appreciation blew away his last restraint and his art's power took absolute command of his soul.

"You couldn't help feeling terrific," Harold said, and a curiously mixed look of embarrassment and victorious pleasure flushed his face. "I mean, once you saw Hitler in the throes, he was like . . . I don't know . . . a girl. I know it sounds crazy, but he almost looked delicate, in a kind of monstrous way." I thought he was dissatisfied with this explanation, but he broke off and said, "Anyway, we had them all in the palm of our hands and it felt goddam wonderful, after being scared half to death." And he gave a little empty laugh that I couldn't quite interpret.

The routines, repeated three times at the order of the more and more involved Leader, took close to two hours to finish. As the troupe took bows, Hitler, eyes shining, rose from his chair and gave them a two-inch nod, his accolade, then sat, his chaste authority descending upon him again. Fugler and he now busily whispered together. The room fell silent. No one knew what to do. The retinue picked at the tablecloths and sipped water, staring about aimlessly. On the stage, the troupe stood, shifting from hip to hip. Worth, after several minutes, started to walk away in a silent show of defiance, but Bix rushed to him and led him back to the others. Hitler was clearly impassioned with Fugler, time and again pointing at Harold, who stood waiting with the troupe a few feet away. The dancers' hands were clasped behind their backs. Carol Conway, terrified, kept defensively nodding, coquettishly lifting and lowering her eyebrows toward the uniformed men, who gallantly smiled back.

More than ten minutes had gone by when Fugler gestured to Harold to join them at the table. Fugler's hand was trembling, his lips cracked with dryness, his eyes stared like a sleepwalker's; Harold saw in the man's tremendous success tonight the volcanic power Hitler wielded, and once again was touched by fear and pride at having tamed it. "You could laugh at him from a distance," Harold said of Hitler, "but up close, let me tell you, you felt a lot better off if he liked you." In his adolescent face I began to see something like anguish as he smiled at his remark.

Fugler cleared his throat and faced Harold, his manner distinctly formal. "We shall speak further in the morning, but Herr Hitler wishes to propose to you that . . ." Fugler paused, said Harold, to compose the Leader's message carefully in his mind. Hitler, slipping on a pair of soft brown leather gloves, watched him with a certain excited intensity. "In principle, he wishes you to create a school here in Berlin to teach German people how to tap-dance. This school, as he envisions it, would be set up under a new government department which he hopes you will take charge of until you have trained someone to take your place. Your dancing has deeply impressed him. He believes that the combination it offers of vigorous healthy exercise, strict discipline, and simplicity would be excellent for the well-being of the population. He foresees that hundreds, perhaps thousands, of Germans could be dancing together at the same time, in halls or stadiums, all over the country. This would be inspiring. It would strengthen the iron bonds that unify the German people while raising up their health standards. There are other details, but this is the gist of the Leader's message."

With which Fugler, with military sternness, indicated to Hitler that he had finished, and Hitler stood and offered his gloved hand to Harold, who scrambled to his feet, too nervous to say anything at all. Hitler took a step away from the table, but then, with a sudden bird-like snap of his head, turned back to Harold, and with pursed lips smiled at him and left, his small army behind him, their boots thrumming on the wooden floor.

Telling this, Harold May was, of course, laughing at times, but at other times one could see that he still had not quite shed the awesome distinction implicit in the story. Hitler at the time of the telling was only two years dead, and his menace, which had hung over us all for more than a decade, had not completely disappeared. His victims, so to speak, were still in fresh graves. Repulsive as he had been, and grateful as all of us were for his death, his presence was like a disease we had had to focus on for too long for it to heal and vanish so quickly. That he had been human enough to lose himself in Harold's performance, and had even had artistic aspirations, was not a comfortable thought, and I listened with a certain uneasiness as Harold pushed on with the tale. He looked different now than he had at the start, seeming almost to have aged in the telling of the story.

"Fugler showed up for breakfast again next morning," Harold said, "a totally changed man. The fucking Führer had offered me a *department*! In *person*! And my hit had also raised Fugler a couple of notches in the hierarchy, because the whole audition had been his idea. So the both of us were super *hoch,* big shots. He had a hard time staying in his seat as we went over the next steps. I would have the pick of Berlin spaces for the school, since my authority came directly from the top, and somebody from some other department would shortly be coming by to discuss my salary, but he thought at least fifteen thousand a year was possible. I nearly fell over. A Cadillac was around a thousand in those days. Fifteen was immense money. I had blasted the ball out of the park."

With a school and immense money on offer, he was handed a dilemma, he went on. He could, of course, simply leave the country. But that would mean tossing away enough money to buy himself a house and a car and maybe seriously think about finding a girl and marrying. He now began trying to explain himself more deeply. "I've always had a hard time with major decisions," he said to me, "and of course Hitler'd been in office only a few years and the real truth about the camps and all hadn't hit us yet, although what was already known was bad enough. Not that I'm excusing myself, but I just couldn't honestly say yes or no. I mean, going back to the Balkans wasn't exactly Hollywood, and knocking around in the States again was something I didn't want to think about."

"You mean you accepted the offer?" I asked, smiling in embarrassment.

"I didn't do anything for a couple of days except walk a lot in the city. And nobody was bothering me. My people were enjoying Berlin and, I don't know, I guess I was busy full time trying to figure myself out. I mean, if you were walking around in Berlin just then nothing was happening. It was no different from London or Paris except that it was cleaner. And maybe you'd notice a few more uniformed men here and there." He looked directly at me. "I mean, that's just how it was," he said.

"I understand," I said. But Hitler was too horrible a figure; I couldn't appreciate even the most perverse attraction to him or his Berlin. And it could be that that thought was what made me ask myself for the first time whether Harold had done something utterly outrageous, like . . . falling in love with the monster?

Harold stared out at the street through the drugstore window. I had the feeling that he hadn't quite realized how the story would sound to others. It was partly the particular character of the late forties; for some, but by no means for everyone, there was still an echo of wartime anti-Fascist heroism in the air; on Paris street corners, stone tablets were still being cemented into buildings, commemorating the heroism of some anti-Nazi Frenchman or -woman who had been shot on the spot by Germans. But of course most people, Harold probably among them, were oblivious of these ceremonies and their moral and political significance.

"Go ahead," I said. "What happened next? It's a great story." I reassured him as warmly as I could.

He seemed to open a bit to my acceptance. "Well," he said, "about four or five days later, Fugler showed up again."

Fugler was still in the glow. Talks were proceeding about how and where to set up the school. "Then," said Harold, "without making anything much of it, he told me that of course part of the routine was that every man in an executive cultural position had to pass a 'racial certification program.'" Returning to his ironical grin, Harold said, "I had to get measured for Aryan." He was to accompany Fugler to a Professor Martin Ziegler's laboratory for a routine check.

With this news, Harold found himself drifting into an even more uncomfortable position. "It's hard to explain; I'd ended up in this deal where I knew I'd be having to leave Germany. Exactly when and how I wasn't sure. But being examined seemed to put me in a different position. Because I'd be deceiving them. I mean, they could cook that into a stew, claiming that I was an enemy and they had to do something about me, passport or no passport. I'd gotten so I could smell violence in the air."

But he did not flee. "I don't know," he replied when I asked him why. "I guess I was just waiting to see what would happen. And, look, I don't deny it, the money'd dug itself into my head. Although—" Again he broke off, dissatisfied with that explanation.

In any case, as he got into Fugler's car he began to fear that he might be even more vulnerable because he had come to Hitler's personal and affectionate notice. "It was almost like . . . I don't know, like he was watching me. Maybe because we'd met, I'd shaken his actual hand," he said, suggesting that he also had a vague feeling of obligation to Hitler, who, after all, was his would-be benefactor—whom he had misled.

Watching Harold now, I found things simplified; there was certainly a bewildering mix of feelings in him, but I thought I saw a clear straight line underneath—Hitler had esteemed him so feelingly, in a sense had loved him or at least his talent, and more ardently than anyone anywhere else had ever come close to equalling. I wondered if that performance had been the high point of his art, perhaps of his life, a hook he had swallowed that he could still not cough up. After all, he had never become a star and probably would never again feel the burning heat of that magical light upon his face.

In the car, sitting beside Fugler on the way to his exam, and looking through the window at the great city and the ordinary things people did on the street, Harold felt that everything he saw seemed to signify, was suddenly like a painting, as though it were all supposed to *mean* something. But what? "You had to wonder," he said, "did they all feel like this? Like they were in a fishbowl and up above there was somebody looking down who *cared*?"

I couldn't believe my ears—Hitler *cared*?

Harold's eyes now were filled. He said that when he looked at Fugler sitting comfortably beside him smoking his English cigarette, and then at the people on the streets, "everything was so fucking *normal*. Maybe that's what was so frightening about it. Like you're drowning in a dream and people are playing cards on the beach a few yards away. I mean, here I'm in a car going to have my nose measured or something, or my cock inspected, and this was absolutely normal, too. I mean, these were not some fucking moon people, these people had *refrigerators*!"

Anger seemed to speak in him for the first time, but not, I thought, at the Germans particularly. It was, rather, at some transcendent situation that was beyond defining. Of course, his nose was small, a pug nose, and circumcision had become common among Germans by that time, so he had little to fear from a physical examination. And, as though reading my thought, he added, "Not that I was afraid of an exam, but . . . I don't know . . . that I was *involved* with this kind of shit—" He broke off again, again dissatisfied with his explanation, I thought.

The walls of Eugenics Professor Ziegler's inner office, in a modern building, were loaded with heavy medical volumes and plaster casts of heads—Chinese, African, European—on shelves behind sliding glass. Glancing around, Harold felt surrounded by an audience that had died. The Professor himself was on the tiny side, a nearsighted, rather obsequious scholar, hardly up to Harold's armpits, who hurriedly ushered him to a chair while Fugler waited in the outer office. The Professor tick-tacked around on the white linoleum floor gathering notebook, pencils, and fountain pen, while assuring Harold, "Only a few minutes and we can finish. Indeed, this is quite exciting, your school."

Now, sitting down on a high stool facing Harold, notebook on his lap, the Professor noted the satisfactory blue of his eyes and the blond hair, turned his palms up, apparently looking for a telltale sign of something, and finally announced, "We shall take some measurements, please." Drawing a large pair of brass calipers out of his desk drawer, he held one side under Harold's chin and the other on the crown of his head, and noted down the distance between them. The same with the width of his cheekbones, the height of his forehead from the bridge of his nose, the width of his mouth and jaws, the length of his nose and ears, and their positions relative to the tip of his nose and crown of his head. Each span was carefully plotted in a leather-bound notebook, as Harold sat trying to think of how to get hold of a railroad timetable without being noticed, and how to create an unobjectionable reason for having to go to Paris that very evening.

The whole session had taken about an hour, including an inspection of his penis, which, though circumcised, was of little interest to the Professor, who, with one eyebrow critically raised, had bent forward to look at the member for a moment, "like a bird with a worm in front of him." Harold laughed. Finally, looking up from the notes spread out on his desk, the Professor announced with a decided clink of professional self-appreciation in his voice, "I am concluding zat you are a very strong and distinct type of the Aryan race, and I wish to offer you my best wishes for suczess."

Fugler, of course, had never had any doubts on this score, especially not now, when he was being credited by the regime as the creator of this astonishing program. Imitating Fugler's smooth accent, Harold told how, on the way back in the car, he had become rhapsodic about tap's promising to "transform

Germany into a community not only of producers and soldiers but artists, the noblest and most eternal spirits of humanity," and so on. Turning to Harold beside him, he said, "I must tell you—but may I call you Harold now?"

"Yes. Sure."

"Harold, this adventure—if I may call it so—coming to such a triumphant conclusion, suggests to me what an artist must feel when finishing a composition or painting or any work of art. That he has immortalized himself. I hope I am not embarrassing you."

"No—no. I see what you mean," Harold said, his mind distinctly elsewhere.

Back in the hotel, Harold greeted the members of his troupe who had gathered in his room. He was quite pale and frightened. He sat the three dancers down and said, "We're getting out."

Conway said, "Are you all right? You look white."

"Pack. There's a train at five tonight. We have an hour and a half. My mother is very ill in Paris."

Benny Worth's eyebrows went up. "Your mother's in *Paris*?" Then he caught Harold's look, and the three dancers rose and without a word hurried out to their rooms to pack.

As Harold expected, Fugler was not giving up that easily. "The desk clerk must have called him," Harold said, "because we had hardly turned in our keys when there he was, looking around at our luggage with disaster in his face."

"What are you doing? You can't possibly be leaving," Fugler said. "What has happened? There is a definite possibility of a dinner with the Führer. This is not to be declined!"

Conway, who happened to be standing nearby, stepped over to Fugler. Fright had raised her voice half an octave. "Can't you see? He's terrified of his mother's passing away. She's not an old woman, so something terrible must have happened."

"I can call the Paris embassy. They will send someone. You must stay! This is impossible! What is her address? Please, you must give me her address, and I will see that doctors attend to her. This cannot happen, Mr. May! Herr Hitler has never before in his life expressed such . . ."

"I'm Jewish," Harold said.

"What did he say?" I asked, astonished.

Harold looked up, caught up in my excitement. I wondered then if this was the point of the story—to describe his escape not only from Germany but from his relation to Hitler, such was the pleasure spreading over his grinning boy's face, right up to the part in the middle of his hair.

"Fugler said, 'How do you do?'"

"How do you do!" I almost yelled, totally flummoxed.

"That's what he said. 'How do you do?' He took half a step back like a shot of compressed air had hit him in the chest, and said, 'How do you do?' and stuck out his hand. His mouth fell open. He went white. I thought he was going to faint or shit. I felt a little sorry for him. . . . I even shook his hand. And I saw he was scared, like he'd seen a ghost."

"What did he mean, 'How do you do'?" I demanded.

"I've never been sure," Harold said, seriously now. "I've thought about it a lot. He had an expression like I'd dropped down from the ceiling in front of him. And definitely scared. Definitely. I mean badly scared. Which I could understand, because he'd brought a Jew in front of Hitler. Jews to them were like a disease, which is something I didn't really understand till later. But I think it could have been something else that had him frightened, too."

He paused for a moment, staring at his empty soda glass. Through the window I saw office workers starting to crowd the sidewalk; the day was ending. "Thinking back to when we met in Budapest and all, I wonder if maybe he'd gotten to, you know, feel pretty close to me. I don't mean sex, I mean like I'd been his ticket to that face-to-face with Hitler, which only important people ever got to have, and on top of that I know he had a top spot in the new school marked out for himself. I mean, I'd gotten hold of the power in a certain way, which I'd begun to notice when I was taken to the Professor to be certified and in the car Fugler began treating me as though I were higher up than him. And when the Professor came out and told him I was kosher, he was already turning into a different man, like he was under me. It was sort of pathetic.

"Mind you," Harold went on, "this was before we knew much about the camps and all," and then he stopped.

"What do you mean?" I asked.

"Nothing. Just that I . . ." He broke off. After a moment, he looked at me and said, "To tell the truth, he wasn't really such a bad guy, Fugler. Just crazy. Badly crazy. They all were. The whole country. Maybe all countries, frankly. In a way. When I look at Berlin bombed to shit now, everything on the ground, and I remember it when there wasn't a candy wrapper on the sidewalks, and you ask yourself, How is this possible? What did it to them? Something did it. What was it?"

He paused again. "I'm not excusing them in any way, but when he said, 'How do you do?' as though he'd never seen me before, I thought, These people are absolutely in a dream. And suddenly here's this Jew who he'd thought was a person. I guess you could say it was a dream that killed forty million people, but it was still a dream. To tell the truth, I think we all are—in a dream, I mean. I've kept thinking that ever since I left Germany. It's over ten years since I got home, and I'm still wondering about it. I mean, no people love nuts and bolts like Germans. Practical people down to their shoelaces. But they still dreamed themselves into this rubble."

He glanced out at the street. "You can't help wondering, when you walk around in the city. Are we any different? Maybe we're also caught in some dream." And, gesturing toward the crowd moving along the street, he said, "The things in their heads, the things they believe. Who knows how real it is? To me now we're like walking songs, walking novels, and the only time it gets to seem real is when somebody kills somebody." No one spoke for a moment; then I asked, "So you got out all right?"

"Oh, no problem. They were probably glad to see us go without bad publicity. We went back to Budapest and then we worked the wheel till the Germans marched into Prague, and after that we came home." He sat back in his chair, preparing to stand. It struck me how deceptively young and unmarked he had seemed a half hour earlier, when we first met, like a guy fresh out of the Corn Belt, while in fact failure had wrinkled the flesh around his eyes. He stuck out his hand, and I shook it. "Use it if you like," he said. "I want people to know. Maybe you'll figure it out—be my guest." Then he got up and went out into the street.

I never saw him again, but the story has visited me a hundred times over the past fifty years, and for some reason I keep pushing it under again. Maybe I would much rather think of positive, hopeful things. Which could also be a way of dreaming, of course. Still, I like to think that a lot of good things have come out of dreaming.

BEAVERS

The pond, normally as silent as a glass of water, now gave up a sound, a splash at the man's approach. A heavy splash far weightier than a frog or leaping fish could make. And then spread itself flat as the mirror it usually was. The man waited but there was only silence. He walked the shoreline watching for signs, stood still listening. His eye caught the tree stump at the far end of the pond. Coming upon it, he saw the fallen poplar and its gnawed tip and the gnawed stump as well. He had beavers. Strangers thieving his privacy. Now, scanning the shore, he counted six trees felled during the single night. In another twenty-four hours the slope above the pond would begin to look like wasteland. Another couple of days and a bulldozer would seem to have gone through it, knocking over what was a lovely wood that had nestled the pond through the years. Long ago he had marveled at the wreckage of a wood on Whittlesy's place, at least ten acres looking like the Argonne Forest after a World War I shelling. The green woods at his back were his to defend.

He turned back to the water in time to see the flattened rodent head moving across the water. Watched motionless as the beast arrived at the narrow end of the pond and sounded, its flat leathery tail, with a parting slap on the water, flashing toward the sky as it slipped down and disappeared. Stepping closer to the shoreline, the man now made out, just below the surface of the clear, sky-reflecting water, the outline of the lodge. Incredible. They must have built it overnight, since he had been swimming right there the day before and there had been nothing. Amazement chilled his spine, the sheer appropriation. He recalled reading, long ago, that beaver shit was toxic. He and Louisa could no longer swim here as they had for thirty years, exulting in the water's purity, which had once tested potable, cleansed by its passage upward through sand and clay.

He hurried up to the house and found his shotgun and a box of shells and hurried back down the hill to the pond and circled around it to the lodge. With the sun lower he could make out its structure, a wall woven of thin branches the beaver had cut from the trees it had felled and then plastered with mud from the pond's bottom. Most likely the animal was resting on the shelf it had built inside the structure. The man aimed, careful to miss the lodge, and fired into the water's surface, which answered with a resonating boom and a peppering of light. The man waited. In a few minutes the head appeared. Expecting a confrontation, he reloaded and waited, hoping not to kill the beast but to introduce it to enough uncertainty to make it go away. He fired again. The flat tail arched up and sounded. The man waited. In a few minutes the head reappeared. The beaver swam, possibly worried but showing full confidence as it headed in a straight line across the pond to the fourteen-inch steel overflow pipe that stood five or six feet in from the opposite shore. There, defiantly—or was it some other emotion?—the beast pulled down a hazel bush growing at the shoreline and swam with it in its jaws and, raising up, pushed the whole plant into the pipe. Then it dived and emerged again with a tangle of grass and mud in its grasp and shoved that load into the pipe on top of the hazel bush. He was intending to stop the overflow. He wanted to raise the water level of the pond.

Perplexed, the man, standing across the pond from this intense work, sat on his heels to think about the enigma before him. The conventional analysis was that beaver dam building had as its purpose the blocking of a small stream with a dam in order to create a pond in which the beaver could build its lodge and raise its family, safe from predators. The project would deforest large areas that provided thin branches for lodge building, and cellulose from the felled tree stems on which the animal lived. *But this fellow already had a deep pond in which to build its lodge.* Indeed, it had already built one. Why did it need to stuff the pipe, stop the overflow, and raise the pond level? The whole effort was somehow admirable for its engineering skill and, in this case, thoroughly pointless. Watching the beast working, the man recognized his feeling of unhappiness with what he was witnessing and wondered, after a few minutes, whether he had somehow come to rely on nature as an ultimate source of steady logic and order, which only senseless humans betrayed with their greed and frivolous stupidity. This beaver was behaving like an idiot, imagining he was creating a pond where a perfect one already existed. The man aimed close enough to the beast to remind him once again of his unwelcome, fired, saw the tail rise and slap the water, and the idiot was gone.

In a few minutes he had surfaced and returned to stuffing the pipe. The man felt himself weakening before this persistence, this absolute dedication that was so unlike his own endlessly doubting nature, his fractured convictions. He would need some expert advice; one way or another the beast had to go.

Carl Mellencamp, the druggist's son, was the man he needed. He had known Carl since his infancy, watched him grow enormous until now, in his late twenties, when he stood over six feet tall, weighing probably well over two hundred, with a rocking gait, thick archer's fists, a steady mason's gaze, and a certain straw hat with curled-up brim that he had worn cocked to the left side in heat and snow for at least the last ten years or maybe more. Carl lived to lay up stone walls, install verandas and garden paths, and hunt with gun or bow. When he arrived in his white Dodge truck late in the afternoon, the man felt the heavy cloak of responsibility passing off his shoulders and onto Carl's.

They went first to inspect the pipe, Carl carrying his rifle. Through the clear water they saw, with some amazement, that the beast had piled up a cone of mud around it reaching up to its lip. "He's got in mind to seal that pipe good and solid."

"But why the hell is he doing it? He's already got a pond," the man said.

"You might ask him next time you see him. We're going to have to kill him. And his wife."

The man stood there on the top of the dam shaking his head. "Isn't there some way to scare him off? . . . And I haven't seen a wife."

"She's around," Carl said. "They're juveniles, probably, that got thrown out of the tribe in Whittlesy's pond. Maybe two or three years old. They go forth to start a new family. They mean to stay." And waving his arm toward a stand of pines at the far end of the pond that the man had planted as seedlings four decades earlier, he said, "You can kiss a lot of those trees goodbye."

"I'd hate to kill them," the man said.

"I don't like it either," Carl said, and stood there squinting down at the water. Then he straightened up and said, "Let me try pissing."

The sun was almost down, long shadows stretched toward the pond, the sky's blue was darkening. Carl set off down the length of the dam to where the lodge was and stood pissing on the ground near it. Then he returned to the man and stood shaking his head. "I doubt it'll work. They've got too much invested in that lodge." They heard the splash and saw, down at the end of the pond, that the beast—or one of them—was climbing up out of the water and making his way a few feet from where Carl had pissed, undeterred by the scent of man.

"So much for that," Carl whispered. "I'd like to get him when he's out of the water, OK?"

The man nodded. The hateful stabbing joy of the kill moved into him. "Incidentally," he asked with an ironical smile, "are we legal?"

"As of this year," Carl said. "They've finally decided they're pests."

"What about trapping them?"

"I don't have traps. And what would we do with them? Nobody wants them. I know a guy would take the pelt, but they're not protected anymore."

"Well, OK," the man agreed.

"Don't move," Carl whispered, and lowered himself to one knee, raising the rifle to his shoulder and cocking it as he aimed at the beast climbing up the side of the dam. Suddenly it turned and scurried down the slope it had been climbing and slid into the water. Carl stood up again.

"How'd he know?" the man asked.

"Oh, they know," Carl said with some odd hunter's pride in the beaver's wit. "Stay here and try not to move." He spoke quietly, conspiratorially. "I don't want to hit him in the water or we'll lose him if he sinks," he said. Then he took off down the length of the dam, to the far end, where the lodge was, setting his feet down flat lest he kick a stone and alarm the beasts, the rifle balanced tenderly in his hand.

Facing the lodge there was a dense clump of reeds at the water's edge, some of them rooted under the water. Carl carefully slipped himself into their midst and sat on his heels, the rifle butt resting on his thigh. The man stood watching from the center of the dam, fifty yards away, wondering how Carl could know that the beast would emerge. Carl, he was somehow glad to have learned, had not really wished to kill.

Minutes passed. The man stood watching. Now Carl, he saw through the reeds, was raising his gun very slowly. The shot's reverberations boomed across the water. Carl quickly stepped into the shallow water and lifted the beast, carrying it out of the reeds by the tail. The man hurried to see it. Carl, holding his rifle in his right hand, held the dead thing up to him with his left and then, suddenly dropping it onto the grass, turned back toward the pond, raised his gun and fired toward the op-

posite shore. "That was the lady," he said, and, handing his gun
to the man, hurried down the dam and around the end of the
pond and halfway up the other side, where he reached down
into the water and lifted out the beaver's mate.

In the driveway, with the two dead things on the bed of the
truck, the man watched Carl stroking the fur of one of them.
"My friend's going to make something out of these. They're
beauties."

"I don't understand what they had in mind, do you?"

Carl liked leaning on things and raised a foot to rest it on
the hub of a rear wheel, removing his beloved straw hat to
scratch his perspiring scalp. "They had some idea, I guess. It's
like people, you know. Animals are. They have imaginations.
These probably had some imaginary idea."

"He already had a pond. What was the point?" the man
asked.

Carl did not seem overly concerned about the question. He
did not seem to think it was up to him to find a solution to it.

The man pressed on. "I wonder if he was just reacting to the
sound of running water coming out of the pipe."

Amused, Carl said, "Hey. Could be." But he obviously did
not believe this.

"In other words," the man said, "maybe there was no connection between stuffing the pipe and raising the pond level."

"Could be," Carl said, seriously now. "Specially when he'd
already built his lodge. That is peculiar."

"Maybe running water irritates them. They don't like the
sound. Maybe it hurts their ears."

"That would be funny, wouldn't it. And us thinking they do it for a purpose." He was beginning to take to the idea.

"Maybe they don't have any purpose," the man said, excited by the prospect. "They just stop up the sound, and then turn around and see that the water is rising. But in their minds there's no connection between one thing and the other. They just see the pond rising and that gives them the idea of building a lodge in it."

"Or maybe they just don't have anything to do, so they stuff a pipe."

"Right." They both laughed.

"They do one thing," Carl said, "and that leads them to do the next thing."

"Right."

"Sounds good to me," Carl said, and opened the truck door and heaved his bulk into the cab. He looked down at the man through the side window. "Story of my life," he said, and laughed. "I started out to be a teacher, you know."

"I remember," the man said.

"Then I fell in love with cement. And next thing you know I'm heaving rocks all over the place."

The man laughed. Carl drove off, waving back through the window. On his truck bed the two beasts' bodies wobbled under their fur.

The man returned to the pond. It was his again, undisturbed. Moonlight was spreading over its silent face like a pale salve. Tomorrow he would have to somehow drag the debris up out of the pipe and get somebody with a backhoe with a long enough reach to extend from the shore over the water and lift the lodge out of the mud it was anchored in.

He sat on the wooden bench he had built long ago beside the little sandy beach where they always entered for a swim. He could hear the water trickling over the drainpipe's edge through the debris the beast had stuffed it with.

What had been in its mind? The question was like a hangnail. Or did it have a mind? Was it merely a question of irritated eardrums? If it had a mind it could imagine a future. It might have had happy feelings, feelings of accomplishment when stuffing the pipe, picturing a rising level of water resulting from its efforts.

But what useless, foolish work! It seemed a contradiction of Nature's economy, which did not allow for silliness, any more than, let's say, a priest or a rabbi or a president or a pope. These types did not take time out to tap-dance or whistle tunes. Nature was serious, he thought, not comical or ironical. After all, a sufficiently deep pond was already there. How could the beast have ignored this? And why, he wondered, was it so disturbing to think about; was it its parallel with his sense of human futility? The more he thought about it the more likely it seemed that the beast had had emotions, a personality, even ideas, not merely blind overpowering instincts that drove it to an act that had completely lost its point.

Or was there some hidden logic here that he was too literal-minded to grasp? Could the beast have had a completely different impulse than the raising of the water level? But what? What could it have been?

Or could he have had nothing in his mind at all except a

muscular happiness at being young and easily able to do what millions of years had trained his mind to do? Beavers, he knew, were extremely social. Once having stuffed the pipe, he may have imagined returning to his mate asleep in the lodge to signal that he had caused the water level to rise. She may have expressed some appreciation. It was something she had always wanted from him for her greater safety. Nor would it occur to her, any more than it had to him, that the water level was already deep enough. The important thing was the idea itself. Of love perhaps. Animals did love. Could he have been stuffing the pipe for love? Real love had no purpose, after all, beyond itself.

Or was it all much simpler: did he simply wake one morning and with infinite pleasure start swimming through the clear water when, quite by chance, he heard the trickling of the overflow and, steering himself over to it, was filled with desire to capture the lovely wet sound, for he adored water above all things and wished somehow to become part of it, if only by capturing its tinkle?

And the rest, as it turned out, was unforeseen death. He had not believed in his death. The shots fired into the water had not caused him to flee but merely to dive and surface again a couple of minutes later. He was young and immortal to himself.

The man, unsatisfied, lingered by the water, tiring of the whole dilemma. Relieved that his woods would not be ravaged nor his water poisoned by beaver crap, he knew he did not regret the killings, sad as they were, despite the animals' complexity and a certain beauty. But he would really have been grateful had he been able to find some clean purpose to the stuffing of the overflow. Anything like that seemed not to exist now, unless its secret had died with the beavers, an idea that oppressed him. And he fantasized about how much more pleasantly things would have turned out had there been not a finished pond to start with but the traditional narrow meandering brook that the beast, in its wisdom, had dammed up in order to create a broad pond deep enough for the construction of its lodge. Then, with the whole thing's utility lending it some daylight sense, one might even have been able to look upon the inevitable devastation of the surrounding trees with a more or less tranquil soul, and somehow mourning him would have been a much more straightforward matter, even as one arranged to shoot him dead. Would something at least feel finished then, completely comprehended and somehow simpler to forget?

THE BARE
MANUSCRIPT

Carol Mundt lay on the desk, propped up on her elbows, reading a cooking article in *You.* She was six feet tall and a hundred and sixty pounds of muscle, bone, and sinew, with only a slightly bulging belly. In Saskatchewan she had not stood out for her size, but here in New York it was a different story. She shifted to take the pressure off her pelvis. Clement said, "Please," and she went still again. She could hear his speeded-up breathing over the back of her head and now and then a soft little sniffing.

"You can sit up now if you like," Clement said. She rolled onto her side and swivelled up to a sitting position, her legs dangling. "I need a few minutes," he said, and added jokingly, "I have to digest this," and laughed sweetly. Then he went over to his red leather armchair, which faced the dormer window that looked uptown as far as Twenty-third Street. Sighing, getting comfortable in his chair, he stared over the sunny rooftops. The house was the last remaining brownstone on a block of old converted warehouses and newish apartment houses. Carol let her head hang forward to relax, sensing that she was not to speak at such moments, then slid off the desk, her buttocks making a zipping sound as they came unstuck from the wood, and crossed the large study to the tiny bathroom, where she sat studying a recipe in the *Times* for meat loaf. Three or four minutes later, she heard "OK!" through the thin bathroom door, and hurried back to the desk, where she stretched out prone, this time resting her cheek on the back of one hand, and closed her eyes. In a moment, she felt the gentle movement of the marker on the back of her thigh and tried to imagine the words it was making. He started on her left buttock, making short grunts that conveyed his rising excitement, and she kept herself perfectly still to avoid distracting him, as if he were operating on her. He began writing faster and faster, and the periods and the dots over the "i"s pushed deep into her flesh. His breathing was louder, reminding her again what a privilege it was to serve genius in this way, to help a writer who, according to his book jacket, had won so many prizes before he was even thirty and was possibly rich, although the furniture didn't match and had a worn look. She felt the power of his mind like the big hand pressing down on her back, like a real object with weight and size, and she felt honored and successful and congratulated herself for having dared answer his ad.

Clement was now writing on the back of her calf. "You can read, if you like," he whispered.

"I'm just resting. Is everything OK?"

"Yes, great. Don't move."

He was down around her ankle when the marker came to a halt. "Please turn over," he said.

She rolled onto her back and lay looking up at him.

He stared down at her body, noting the little smile of embarrassment on her face. "You feeling all right about this?"

"Oh, yes," she said, in this position nearly choking on her high automatic laugh.

"Good. You're helping me a lot. I'll start here, OK?" He touched just below her solid round breasts.

"Wherever," she said.

Clement pushed up his wire-rimmed glasses. He was half a head shorter than this giantess, whose affectionate guffaws, he supposed, were her way of hiding her shyness. But her empty optimism and that damned Midwestern affliction of regular-fella good will annoyed him, especially in a woman—it masculinized her. He respected decisive women, but from a distance, much preferring the inexplicit kind, like his wife, Lena. Or, rather, like Lena as she once was. He would love to be able to tell this one on his desk to relax and let her bewildered side show, for he had grasped her basic tomboy story and her dating dilemmas the moment she'd mentioned how she'd had her own rifle up home and adored hunting deer with her brothers Wally and George. And now, he surmised, with her thirties racing toward her, the joke was over but the camouflaging guffaws remained, like a shell abandoned by some animal.

With his left hand, he slightly stretched the skin under her breast so that the marker could glide over it, and his touch raised her eyebrows and produced a slightly surprised smile. Humanity was a pitiful thing. An inchoate, uncertain joy was creeping into him now; he had not felt this kind of effortless shaping in his sentences since his first novel, his best, which had absolutely written itself and made his name. Something was happening in him that had not happened in years: he was writing from the groin.

Self-awareness had gnawed away at his early lyricism. His reigning suspicion was simply that his vanishing youth had taken his talent with it. He had been young a very long time. Even now his being young was practically his profession, so that youthfulness had become something he despised and could not live without. Maybe he could no longer find a style of his own because he was afraid of his fear, and so instead of brave sentences that were genuinely his own he was helplessly writing hollow imitation sentences that could have belonged to anybody. Long ago he had been able to almost touch the characters his imagining had provided, but slowly these had been replaced by a kind of empty white surface like cold, glowing granite or a gessoed canvas. He often thought of himself as having lost a gift, almost a holiness. At twenty-two, winner of the Neiman-Felker Award, and, soon after, the Boston Prize, he had quietly enjoyed an anointment that, among other blessings, would prevent him, in effect, from ever growing old. After some ten years of marriage, he began groping around for that blessing in women's company, sometimes in their bodies. His boyish manner and full head of hair and compact build and ready laughter, but mainly his unthreatening vagueness, moved some women to adopt him for a night, for a week, sometimes for months, until he or they wandered off, distracted. Sex revived him, but only until he was staring down at a blank sheet of paper, when once again he knew death's silence.

To save the marriage, Lena had pointed him toward psycho-analysis, but his artist's aversion to prying into his own mind and risking the replacement of his magic blindness with every-day common sense kept him off the couch. Nevertheless, he had gradually given way to Lena's insistence—her degree had been in social psychology—that his father might have injured him far more profoundly than he had ever dared admit. A chicken farmer in a depressed area near Peekskill, on the Hudson, Max Zorn had a fanatical need to discipline his son and four daughters. Clement at nine, having accidentally beheaded a chicken by shutting a door on its neck, was locked in a windowless potato cellar for a whole night, and for the rest of his life had been unable to sleep without a light on. He had also had to get up to pee two or three times a night, no doubt as a consequence of his terror of peeing on potatoes in the dark. Emerging into the morning light with the open blue sky over his head, he asked his father's pardon. A smile grew on his father's stubbled face, and he burst out laughing as he saw that Clement was pissing in his pants. Clement ran into the woods, his body shaking with chills, his teeth chattering despite the warm spring morning. He lay down on a broken hay bale that was being warmed by the sun and covered himself with the stalks. The experience was in principle more or less parallel to that of his youngest sister, Margie, who in her teens took to staying out past midnight, defying her father. Returning from a date one night, she reached up to the cord hanging from the overhead light fixture in the entrance hall and grasped a still warm dead rat that her father had hung there to teach her a lesson.

But none of this entered Clement's first story, which he expanded into his signature novel. Instead, the book described his faintly disguised mother's adoration of him, and pictured his father as a basically well-meaning, if sad, man who had some difficulty with expressing affection, nothing more. Clement, in general, would always find it hard to condemn; Lena thought that for him the levelling of judgment in itself was a challenge to confront his father and symbolically invited a second entombment. And so his writing was romantically left-wing, a note of wistful protest always trembling in it somewhere, and if this quality of innocence was attractive in his first book it seemed predictably formulaic thereafter. In fact, he would join the sixties' anarchic revolt against forms with enormous relief, having come to despair of structure itself as the enemy of the poetic; but structure in art—so Lena told him—implied inevitability, which threatened to turn him toward murder, the logical response to his father's terrifying crimes. This news was too unpleasant to take seriously, and so in the end he remained a rather lyrical and winningly cheerful fellow, if privately unhappy with his unbudging harmlessness.

Lena understood him; it was easy, since she shared his traits. "We are charter members of the broken-wing society," she said late one night while cleaning up after one of their parties. For a while in their late twenties and thirties, a party seemed to coagulate every weekend in their Brooklyn Heights living room. People simply showed up and were gladly welcomed to smoke their cigarettes, from which Lena snipped off the filters, to flop on the carpet and sprawl on the worn furniture, to drink the wine they'd brought and talk about the new play or movie or novel or poem; also to lament Eisenhower's collapsed syntax, the blacklisting of writers in radio and Hollywood, the mystifying new hostility of blacks toward Jews, their traditional allies, the State Department's lifting of suspect radicals' passports, the perplexing irrational silence that they felt closing in on the country as its new conservatism went about scooping out and flipping away its very memory of the previous thirty years, of the Depression and the New Deal, even changing the war's Nazi enemy into a kind of defender against the formerly allied Russians. Some were refreshed by the Zorns' hospitality and went into the night either newly joined or alone but, either way, under the influence of a forlorn time of lost valor: they saw themselves as a lucid minority in a country where ignorance of the world's revolution was bliss, money was getting easier to make, the psychoanalyst the ultimate authority, and an uncommitted personal detachment the prime virtue.

In due time, Lena, uncertain about everything except that she was lost, analyzed matters and saw that she, like his sentences, was no longer his, and that their life had become what he took to saying his writing had become: an imitation. They went on living together, now in a lower-Manhattan brownstone on permanent loan by the homosexual heir of a steel fortune, who believed Clement was another Keats. But Clement often slept on the third floor these days and Lena on the first. The gift of the house was only the largest of many gifts that people dropped on them: a camel's-hair coat came from a doctor friend who found that he needed a larger size; the use of a cottage on Cape Cod year after year from a couple who went off to Europe every summer, and with it an old but well-maintained Buick. Fate also provided. Walking along a dark street one night, Clement kicked something metallic, which turned out to be a can of anchovies. Bringing it home, he found that it needed a special key and put it in a cupboard. More than a month later, on a different street, he once again kicked metal—the key to the can. He and Lena, both anchovy lovers, instantly broke out some crackers and sat down and ate the whole thing.

They still had some laughs together, but mostly they shared a low-level pain that neither of them had the strength to bring to a head, both feeling they had let the other down. "We even have an imitation divorce," she said, and he laughed and agreed, and they went on anyway with nothing changed except that she cut her long wavy blond hair and took a job as a child counsellor. Despite their never having been able to decide to have a child, she understood children instinctively, and he saw with some dismay that her work was making her happy. At least for a while, she seemed to perk up with some sort of self-discovery, and this threatened to leave him behind. But in less than a year she quit, announcing, "I simply cannot go to the same place every day." This was the return of the old crazy lyrical Lena, and it pleased him despite his alarm at the loss of her salary. They were beginning to need more money than he could make, with the sales of his books falling to near nothing. As for sex, it was hard for her to recall when it had meant very much to her. Gradually, it was a four- or five-times-a-year indulgence, if that. His affairs, which she suspected but refused to confirm, relieved her of a burden even as they gnawed at what was left of her self-regard. His view was that a man had to *go* somewhere with his erection, while a woman felt she *was* somewhere. A big difference. But in a cruel moment he admitted to himself that she was too unhappy to be happily screwed, a condition he blamed on her background.

Then one summer afternoon, while smoking his pipe on the rickety step of their donated beach cottage, he saw a girl walking all alone by the lip of the sea, looking totally immersed in her thoughts, with the sun flashing across her hips, and he imagined how it would be if he could get her naked and write on her. His soul quickened. It had been a long, long time since he had had any vision of himself that brought such a lift of joy. This picture of himself writing on a woman's body was somehow wholesome and healthful, like holding a loaf of fresh bread.

He might never have placed the ad at all had Lena not finally erupted. He was up in his third-floor workroom, reading Melville, trying to cleanse his mind, when he heard screaming from downstairs. Lena, when he rushed into the living room, was sitting on the couch pouring herself into the air. He held her in his arms until she was exhausted. There was no need to talk; she was simply dying of inchoate outrage at her life, the relentless lack of money and his failure to provide some kind of lead. He held her hand, and could hardly bear to look at her ravaged face.

She grew quiet. He brought her a glass of water. They sat together on the couch, waiting for nothing. She took a Chesterfield from a pack on the coffee table, snipped off its filter with her fingernail, and lay back inhaling defiantly, Dr. Saltz having seriously warned her twice now. She was having an affair with Chesterfields, Clement thought.

"I'm thinking of writing something autobiographical," he said, somehow implying that this would bring in money.

"My mother . . ." she said, and went silent, staring.

"Yes?"

This obscure mention of her mother reminded him of the first time she had openly revealed the guilt she felt. They were sitting at Lena's rooming-house window overlooking a splendid street lined with trees in full leaf, with students idling past and the placid quiet of a Midwestern campus sequestering them from the real world, while back in Connecticut, she said, her mother was rising before five every morning to board the first streetcar for her eight-hour day in the Peerless Steam Laundry. Imagine! Noble Christa Vanetzki ironing strangers' shirts so she could send her daughter the twenty dollars a month for room and board, meanwhile refusing to let her daughter work, as most students did. Lena had to shut her eyes and squeeze her unworthiness out of her mind. To make her mother happy, she had to succeed, success would cure everything—maybe a job in social psychology with a city agency.

She was wearing her white angora sweater. "That sweater makes you glow like a spirit in this crazy light," Clement said. They went out for a walk, holding hands along the winding paths through shadows so black they seemed solid. The clarity of the moon that windless night brought it unnervingly near. "It's got to be closer than usual, or something," he said, squinting up at its light. He loved the poetry of science, but the details were too mathematical. In this amazing glare his cheekbones were more prominent and his manly jaw sculpted. They were exactly the same height. She had always known he adored her, but alone with him she could sense his body's demand. Suddenly he drew her into a clearing beneath some bushes and gently pulled her to the ground. They kissed, he fondled her breasts, and then stretched out and pressed against her to spread her legs. She felt his hardness and tensed with the fear of embarrassment. "I can't, Clement," she said, and kissed him apologetically. She had never given even this much of herself to anyone before, and she wanted her gift forgotten.

"One of these days we have to." He rolled off her.

"Why!" She laughed nervously.

"Because! Look what I bought."

He held up a condom for her to see. She took it from him and felt the smooth rubber with her thumb. She tried not to think that all his verses about her—the sonnets, the villanelles, the haiku—were merely ploys to prepare her for this ridiculous rubber balloon. She raised it to her eye like a monocle and looked up at the sky. "I can almost see the moon through it."

"What the hell are you doing!" He laughed and sat up. "The mad Vanetzkis." She sat up giggling and returned the condom to him. "What is it, your mother?" he asked.

She was dead serious. "Maybe you ought to find somebody else. We could still be friends." And then she added, "I really don't understand why I'm alive." Clement had always been moved by these quick mood changes—"the Polish depths," he called them. She had a baffling connection with some mystery across the Atlantic in the dark Polish middle of Europe, a place neither he nor she had ever been.

"Is there a poem about anything like this?"

"Like what?"

"A girl who can't find out what she thinks."

"Probably Emily Dickinson, but I can't think of a particular one. Every love poem I know ends with glory or death."

He wrapped his arms around his raised knees and stared up at the moon. "I've never seen it like this before. This must be how it makes wolves howl."

"And women go mad," she added. "Why is it always women the moon makes mad?"

"Well, they've got such a head start."

She bent forward to clear a branch from her line of sight, narrowing her gaze against the glare. "I really think it could make me crazy." In a distant way, she actually was afraid of insanity. Her father's mad death had never left her. "How close it seems, like an eye in Heaven. I can see it frightening people. You'd think it would be warm with this brightness, but it's cold light, isn't it? Like the light of death." Her dear, child-like curiosity chilled him with anticipation of her body, which he still hoped to have someday. Was she blond down there? At the same time, she was holy and rare. Her only defect was her cheekbones, slightly too prominent but not fatally so, and the too broad Polish nose. But he was past comparing her to perfection. He opened her hand and pressed her palm to his lips. "Cathleen ni Houlihan, Elizabeth Barrett Browning, Queen Mab"—now he had her giggling pityingly—"Betty Grable . . . who else?"

"The Karamazov woman?"

"Ah, yes, Grushenka. And who else? Peter-Paul Mounds, Baby Ruth, Cleopatra . . ." She grasped him by the head and crushed her mouth on his. She hated disappointing him like this, but the more physical she tried to become the less she felt. Maybe if they did do it, some spring would uncoil inside her. He was certainly gentle and lovable, and if anyone was to enter her before she found a husband it might as well be Clement. Or maybe not. She was certain of nothing. She let his tongue slide over hers. Her welcoming mouth surprised him, and he rolled her back and lay on her and began pumping, but she slid out from under him, got up, and walked out onto the path, and he caught up with her and had started to apologize when he saw her intense concentration. Her frustrating mood changes dangled above him like a bright-colored toy over a baby's crib. They walked in a nearly mournful silence to the road and then to her rooming house, where they stood below the deep Victorian porch, the brightness of the moon stretching their giant inky silhouettes across the grass.

"I wouldn't know how to do it."

"I could teach you."

"I'll be embarrassed."

"Only for a minute or two. It's easy." They both burst out laughing. He loved to kiss her laughing mouth. She touched his lips with her fingertips.

He stood on the sidewalk watching her incredible form going up the path to the house—her round ass, the full thighs. She turned in the doorway and waved and vanished.

He had to marry her, crazy as that sounded. But how? He had nothing, not even prospects, unless he could win another prize or be taken on as a faculty assistant. But there were hundreds with degrees higher than his looking for jobs. He was most likely going to lose her. An erection was stirring as he stood there on the moon-flooded sidewalk, a hundred feet from where she was undressing.

"Why do you bother with her?" Mrs. Vanetzki asked Clement. Clyde, the white-and-black mutt, lay stretched out in the shade, dozing at her feet. It was a hot mill-town Sunday afternoon, the last day of spring break. Even the rushing Winship River looked oily and warm below the house, and in the still air shreds of the smoke of a long-departed train hung over the railroad tracks along the riverbank.

"I don't know," Clement said. "I figure she might get rich someday."

"Her? Ha!" For Clement's visit, Mrs. Vanetzki wore a carefully ironed blue cotton dress with lace trim around the collar, and white oxfords. Her reddish hair was swept up to a white comb at the top of her head, emphasizing both her height—she was half a head taller than her daughter—and, somehow, the breadth of her cheekbones and forehead. Beneath her defiant banter, Clement felt the scary force of the majestically defeated, something he could not reconcile with his hopes. A framed tinted photo in the living room showed her only ten years earlier, standing proud beside her husband, with his Byronic foulard and flowing hair, a fedora hanging from his hand. His misunderstanding of America's sometimes lethal contempt for foreignness had not yet strapped him to the stretcher and made him into a paranoid, raving in Polish to the walls of an ambulance, cursing his wife as a whore and the human race as murderers. Only Lena was left her now. The responsible one, "the only one who got herself a brain in her head." Lena's sister

Patsy, the middle child, had had two abortions with different men, one of whose surnames she admitted she didn't know. She had a wild loud whine of a voice and helter-skelter in her eyes. A sweet girl, really, with a big heart, but simply barren in the head. Patsy had once heavily intimated to Clement that she knew Lena was not letting him in and that she would not mind substituting herself "a couple of times." There had been no envy or spite in this offer, simply the fact of it and no hard feelings whichever way he decided. "Hey, Clement, how about me if she won't?" Kidding, of course, except for the undeniable light in her eye.

There was also Steve, the last-born, but for her he somehow hardly counted. He was dull and sweet and heavy-footed, the peasant side of the family. Steve was like Patsy, swimming around like a carp at the bottom of the pond, but at least he wasn't sex-mad. Hamilton Propeller liked him, amazingly enough. They knew they had a serious worker, and had advanced him into calibration technology after his first six months—Steve, who was only nineteen, with but two years of high school. He would be all right, although his recent shenanigans troubled her.

"Steve does a lot of walking in his sleep, you know. Lately." Mrs. Vanetzki addressed this to Lena with an implicit request for her college-educated interpretation.

"Maybe he needs a girl," Lena ventured. Clement was astonished and amused at the irony of her speaking so easily about sex.

"Trouble is there are no whores in this town," Mrs. Vanetzki said, scratching her belly. "Patsy keeps telling him to go to Hartford for a weekend, but he doesn't understand what she's talking about. How about you, Clement?"

"Me?" Clement flushed, imagining she would be asking next if he'd slept with Lena.

"Maybe you could tell him about the birds and bees. I don't think he knows it." Lena and Clement laughed, and Mrs. Vanetzki allowed herself a suppressed grin. "I really don't think he's even heard of it, but what can be done?"

"Well, somebody has to teach him!" Lena exclaimed, worried by her brother's persisting childishness. Clement was baffled that she could apply this level of energy to making her family face their dilemmas when she was fleeing her own.

"He seems to have bent Patsy's old bicycle," Mrs. Vanetzki said, mystified.

"Bent her bicycle!"

"When we were all asleep. He seems to have been sleepwalking in the night and gone outside and bent the front fork in his two hands. It's some kind of force in him." She turned to Clement. "Maybe you could talk to him about going to Hartford some weekend."

But before Clement could reply Mrs. Vanetzki waved him down. "Ah, you men, you never know what to do when it comes to practical."

Lena quickly defended him. "He'd be glad to talk to Steve. Wouldn't you, Clement?"

"Sure, I'd be glad to talk to him."

"But do you know anything about sex?"

"Mama!" Lena went red and screamed with laughter, but her mother barely smiled.

"Oh, I know a thing or two." Clement tried to brush off the woman's bewildering near contempt for him.

"Now, you be nice to Clement, Mama," Lena said, and went and sat on the glider beside her mother.

"Oh, he knows not to be upset. I just say things." But she had pinned inadequacy to his nature. She pushed her heel against the floor and made the glider swing.

Nobody spoke. The glider squeaked intimately. Beyond the porch the street was silent. Mrs. Vanetzki finally turned to Clement. "The main thing that puts people's lives to ruin is sex."

"Oh, come on—even if you love somebody? I love this crazy girl," Clement said.

"Ah, love."

Lena nervously giggled through her cigarette smoke.

"Isn't there such a thing?" Clement asked.

"Whoever is not realistic, America kills," Mrs. Vanetzki said. "You are an educated young man. You are handsome. My daughter is a mixed-up person. She will never change. Nobody changes. Only more and more is let out, that's all, the way a ball of string unwinds. Do yourself a favor—forget about her, or be friends, but don't marry. You should find a smart woman with a practical mind and clear thoughts. Marriage is a thing forever, but a wife is only good if she is practical. This girl has no idea of practical. She is a dreamer, like her poor father. The man comes to this country expecting some respect, at least for his name. Nobody respects a Polack. What did they know of Vanetzkis, who go back to the Lithuanian dukes? He went crazy for a little respect, a man with engineer training. They kept wanting to make friends with him, the kind of people he wouldn't have spoken to in the old country, except maybe to get his shoes shined. So he comes to Akron and Detroit and then here looking for a cultured circle. This is the nature of Lena's father. He didn't know that here you are either a failure or a success, not a human being with a name. So he went raving to his grave. Don't talk about marriage. Please, for both your sakes, leave her to herself. Our Patsy, yes—she should be married. Only marriage can save her, and even that I doubt. But not this one." She turned now to look at her elder daughter, who had giggled in loving embarrassment through all her remarks. "Have you told him how lost you are?"

"Yes," Lena said, uncomfortably. "He knows."

Mrs. Vanetzki sighed, pressed a hand against her own perspiring cheek, and rocked slightly from side to side. She was in touch with what time was to bring to her, Clement thought, and he was moved by this transcendency in her nature, even if it was excessively tragic for his taste.

"What are you going to do for a living? Because I can tell you now she will never amount to anything financially."

"Mama!" Lena protested, delighted by the implied female revolt in her mother's candor. "Oh, Mama, I'm not that bad!"

"Oh, you're getting there," Mrs. Vanetzki said. She repeated her question to Clement. "What are you going to live on?"

"Well, I don't know yet."

"Yet? Don't you know that every day costs money? 'Yet'? Economics does not wait for 'yet.' You have to know what you are going to live on. But I see you are like her—the world is not real to you, either. Isn't there something in Shakespeare about this?"

"Shakespeare?" Clement asked.

"You tell me everything is in Shakespeare. Tell me how a hopeless beautiful girl's supposed to marry a poet who hasn't got a job. My God, you are regular children!" And she laughed, shaking her head helplessly. Clement and Lena, relieved that she was no longer judging them, joined her, delighted that she was sharing their dilemma in this crazy life.

"But it's not going to happen right away, Mother. I've got to graduate first, and then if I can get a job . . ."

"She'll get a job—she's got perfect grades," Clement said, with complete confidence.

"What about you? Is there a job for poets? Why don't you try to be famous? Is there a famous poet in America?"

"Sure, there are famous American poets, but you probably wouldn't have heard of them."

"That's what you call famous, people that nobody's ever heard of?"

"They're famous among other poets and people interested in poetry."

"Write some kind of story—then you'll be famous. Not this poetry. Then maybe they'd make a moving picture out of your story."

"That's not the kind of writing he does, Mama."

"I know, you don't have to tell me that."

Patsy appeared behind the screen door in her bra and panties. "Ma, you seen my other bra?" She sounded persecuted.

"Hangin' up in the bathroom. Why don't you look sometime instead of 'Ma, Ma, Ma'?"

"I did look."

"Well, look again with your eyes open. And when you goin'
to wash your own stuff?"

Patsy opened the screen door and came out barefoot on the
porch, her arms crossed over her big breasts in deference to
Clement. A towel was wrapped like a turban over her wet hair.
In the fading daylight, he saw grandeur in her powerful thighs
and her broad back and deep chest. On an impulse Patsy
grasped her mother's face between her hands and kissed her. "I
love you, Mama!"

"There's a man here and you walking around naked like
that? Go inside, you crazy thing!"

"It's only Clement. Clement don't mind!" She turned her
back on her mother and sister and faced Clement, whose heart
swelled at the sight of her outthrust breasts, barely cupped by
the undersized bra. With her taunting whine of a laugh, she
asked, "You mind me, Clement?"

"No, I don't mind."

Mrs. Vanetzki leaned forward and smacked her daughter's
ass hard with the flat of her hand and then laughed.

"Ow! You hurt me!" Patsy ran into the house, gripping her
buttock.

It was almost dark now. A freight train clanked along in the
near distance. Lena lit a cigarette and leaned back into the
glider cushion.

"He's going to write a play for the stage, Ma."

"Him?"

"He can do it."

"That's good," Mrs. Vanetzki said, as if it were a joke. Before
her black mood of disbelief, everyone fell silent.

Later, they went for a walk. It was a neighborhood of bungalows and four-story wooden apartment houses, workers' homes.

"She's right, I guess," Clement said, hoping Lena would contradict him.

"About getting married?"

"It'd be silly for us."

"Probably," she agreed, relieved. A decision decisively put off was as comforting as one that had been made, and she grasped his hand, lifted by this concretizing of the indefinite.

He could not get up the courage to place the ad. He was beginning to wonder if it might be thought perverse. But it gradually loomed like a duty to himself. One day, he picked up a copy of the *Village Voice* and stood on the corner of Prince and Broadway perusing the personal columns: page after page of randy invitations, pleas for a companion, offers of psychic discovery and physical improvement—like an ice field, he thought, with human voices calling for rescue from deep crevasses. Dante. He took the paper home to his barren desk, trying to think of some strategy, and finally decided on a direct approach: "Large woman wanted for harmless experiment, age immaterial but skin must be firm. Photos."

After five false starts—immensely blubbery nude women photographed from either end—he knew the moment he saw the photo that Carol Mundt was perfect: head thrown back as if in a laughing fit. When she appeared at his door—in her yellow miniskirt and white beret and black blouse, six inches taller than he, and touching in a corny way with that shy, brave grin—he wanted to throw his arms around her, instantly certain that she was going to validate his concept. At last he had done something about his emptiness.

Snuggling into his armchair, she made a desultory attempt to draw down her skirt while trying to look skeptically game, as if they were strangers at a bar. She jingled the heavy bracelets and chains around her neck, and neighed—horse laughter, irritating his sensitive hearing. In fact, there was something virginal about her that she might be working to cover up, maybe extra-virginal, like the best olive oil, a line he resolved to remember to use sometime. "So what's this about? Or am I wide enough?" she asked.

"It's very simple. I'm a novelist."

"Ah-huh." She nodded doubtfully.

He took down one of his books from the shelf and handed it to her. She glanced at his photo on the dust jacket, and her suspicions collapsed. "Well, now, say . . ."

"You will have to be naked, of course."

"Ah-huh." She seemed excited, as if steeling herself for the challenge.

He pressed on. "And I want to be able to write anywhere on you, because, you see, the story I have in mind will need all your space. Although I could be overestimating. I'm not sure yet, but it might be the first chapter of a novel." Then he explained about his block and his hope that writing on her skin would deliver him from its grip. Her eyes widened with fascination and sympathy, and he saw that she was proud to be his confidante. "It may not work—I don't know. . . ."

"Well, it's worth a try, right? I mean, if you don't try you don't fly."

Vamping for time, he moved a small box of paper clips off his desk and a leather-bordered blotter, a long-ago Christmas present from Lena. How to tell her to undress? The madness of the scheme came roaring at him like a wave, threatening to fling him back into his impotence. Scrambling, he said, "Undress, please?"—something he had never actually dared say to a woman, at least not standing up. With what seemed a mere shrug and a wriggle, she was standing before him naked but for her white panties. His eye went down to them and she asked, "Panties?"

"Well, if you don't mind, could you? It's kind of less—I don't know—stimulating with them off, you know? And I want to use that area."

She slid out of her panties and sat on the desk. "Which way?" she asked. Clearly, she had been having compunctions and now in overcoming them had been left in uncertainty, a mental state he practically owned. And so their familiarity deepened.

"On your stomach first. Would you like a sheet?"

"This is all right," she said, and lowered herself onto the desktop. The broad expanse of her tanned back and global white buttocks was in violent contrast, it seemed now, to his desk's former devastated dryness. An engraved silver urn, one of his old prizes, held a dozen felt-tipped pens, one of which he now took in hand. Something in him was quivering with fear. What was he doing? Had he finally lost his mind?

"You OK?" she asked.

"Yes! I'm just thinking."

There had been a story—it was months ago now, maybe a year—which he had begun several times. Then, suddenly and simply, it occurred to him that he had outlived his gift and he had no belief in himself anymore. And now, with this waiting flesh under his hand, he had committed himself to believe again.

"You sure you're OK?" she repeated.

It hadn't been a great story, or even a very good one, but it held the image of how he had first met his wife, under a wave that had knocked them both down and sent them tumbling together toward the beach. As he got to his feet, yanking up his nearly stripped-away trunks while she staggered up as well, pulling her tank suit up over a breast that had popped out in the churning water, he saw them as fated, like Greeks rising from the ocean in some myth of drowning and being reborn.

He was a naïve poet then, and she worshipped Emily Dickinson and burning the candle at both ends. "The sea tried to strip you," he said. "The Minotaur." Her eyes, he saw, were glazed, which pleased him, for he was reassured by vague people, as it soon turned out that she was. Disgorged by the sea—as he saw the scene for years afterward—they instinctively glimpsed in each other the same anguish, the same desire to escape the definite. "Death by the Definite," he would write, a paean to the fog as creative force.

Now, holding the black felt-tipped pen in his right hand, he lowered his left onto Carol's shoulder. The warmth of her firm skin was a shock. Not often had his fantasy turned real, and that she was willing to do this for him, a stranger, threatened tears. The goodness of humanity. He had sensed that she had needed all her courage to respond to his ad, but something kept him from inquiring too deeply about her life. As long as she wasn't crazy. A little weird, maybe, but who wasn't? "Thank you, Carol."

"It's OK. Take your time."

He felt himself beginning to swell. The way it used to happen long, long ago when he wrote. A man wrote with it, his aptly named organ, and a gallon of extra blood seemed to expand his veins. He leaned over Carol's back, his left hand pressing down more confidently on her shoulder now, and slowly wrote: "The wave gathered itself higher and higher far out where the sand shelf dropped down into the depths as the man and the woman tried to swim against the undertow that was sweeping them, strangers to each other, out toward their fate." Astonished, he saw with clarity fragments of days of his youth and young manhood, and, arcing over them like a rainbow, his unquestioning faith in life and its all but forgotten promise. He could smell Carol's flesh as she responded to the pressure of his hand, a green-tinted fecund sea scent that somehow taunted him with his desiccated strength. How to describe the sheer aching he felt in his heart?

And Lena's face rose before him as she had looked more than twenty years before, her eyes slightly bloodshot from the salt water, her swirling blond hair plastered across her laughing face, the fullness of her young body as she stepped upward across the sand and collapsed breathlessly laughing, and himself already in love with her form and both of them somehow familiar and unwary after their shared battering. It seemed that these were the first images he'd experienced in many years, and his pen moved down Carol's back to her buttocks and then down her left thigh and then the right, and, turning her over, it continued onto her chest and belly and then back down her thighs and onto her ankle, where, miraculously, the story, barely disguised, of his first betrayal of his wife came to its graceful end. He felt he had miraculously committed truth to this woman's flesh. But was it a story or the beginning of a novel? Oddly, it didn't matter, but he must show it to his editor right away.

"I finished on your ankle!" he called, surprised by a boyishness in the tone of his voice.

"Isn't that great! Now what?" She sat up, hands childishly spread out in the air so as not to smudge herself.

It struck him how strange it was that she was as ignorant of what had been written on her as a sheet of paper. "I could get you scanned, but I don't have a scanner. Otherwise, I could copy it on my laptop, but it'll take a while—I'm not a fast typist. I just hadn't thought of this . . . unless I put you in a cab to my publisher," he joked. "But I'm only kidding. He might want some cuts."

They solved the problem by him standing behind her reading her back aloud while she sat typing on his laptop. They burst into laughter at the procedure from time to time. For the text on her front, she thought of having a full-length mirror to read from, but it would all be reversed. So he sat down in front of her and typed while she held the machine on her lap. When he had read down to her thighs, she had to stand so he could continue—until he was on the floor reading her calves and ankles.

Then he stood up and they looked deeply into each other's eyes for the first time. Then, possibly because they had done something so intimate, and so unthought-of, they had no idea what to do next, and started to giggle and then collapsed from laughing, an infectious hysteria heaving their diaphragms until they had to lean their foreheads on the edge of the desk and not look at one another. Finally, he was able to say, "You're welcome to shower, if you like." And this for some reason rendered them screeching again, falling around with delicious helplessness.

Gasping, they slid to the floor and their laughter subsided. They lay side by side, filled with some unexpected childish knowledge of one another. Now they were quiet, still panting, lying face-to-face on his Oriental carpet.

"I guess I'll go, right?" she asked.

"How will you wash it off?" he asked, feeling an incomprehensible anxiety.

"Take a bath, I guess."

"But your back . . ."

"I know somebody who'll wash it."

"Who, a man?"

"No, a girl down the hall."

"But I'd rather nobody read it yet. I'm not really sure it's ready to publish, you know? Or for somebody to read it. I mean . . ." He was lurching about, looking for some reason to fend off the curiosity of this unknown back-washing girlfriend;

or perhaps it was to preserve the privacy of his creation—God knew why, but he felt her body was still too personal for any stranger to look at. He raised himself up on one elbow. Her hair had spread out over the carpet. It was almost as if they had made love. "I can't let you out this way," he said.

"What do you mean?" There was a hopeful note in her voice.

"People who know us will recognize things about my wife in it. I'm not ready for that."

"Why'd you write it, then?"

"I just put it down raw and then I'd change some of it later. You can't go this way. I'll take a shower with you and scrub your back, OK?"

"OK, sure. But I didn't intend for anybody to read it," she said.

"I know, but I'll feel better if it's gone."

In the small metal shower stall, she seemed so immense that he started to tire after scrubbing her for a few minutes with his back brush. Carol washed her front, but he did the backs of her thighs, calves, and ankles. And when she was clean, the water coursing down over her shoulders, he drew her to him. There was solid power in her body.

"Feeling better now?" she asked. He went abstract before this woman, the last vestiges of his brain slipping out of his skull and down into his groin.

Later, he wondered why making love to her under the stream of water was so easy and straightforward, while earlier, covered as she was with his words, the very thought of it was like penetrating thick brush and thorns. He wished he could have discussed this riddle with Lena. But of course that was out of the question, although he was not convinced it should be.

After he had helped dry Carol off, she slipped into her panties, bra, and blouse and yanked up her skirt while he sat at the desk and opened a drawer and took out a checkbook. But she immediately touched his wrist.

"It's all right," she said. Her damp hair bespoke their intimacy, the fact that he had changed her.

"But I want to pay you."

"Not this time." An open shyness passed over her face at this perhaps unintended suggestion of her wish to return. "Maybe next time, if you want me again." And then she seemed alarmed by a new thought. "Or will you? I mean, you've done it, right?" Her earlier brashness was returning. "I guess you can't have a first time twice, right?" She laughed softly, but her eyes were imploring.

He stood up and moved in to kiss her goodbye, but she turned away slightly and he landed on her cheek. "I guess you're right," he said.

A certain hardness surfaced in her face now. "Then, look, maybe I'd better take the money."

"Right," he said. Reality is always such a relief, he thought, but why must it come with anger? He sat down and wrote a check and, with a twinge of shame, handed it to her.

She folded the check and stuck it in her purse. "This has been quite a day, hasn't it!" she yelled, and let out one of her horselaughs, startling him, for she had left off laughing like that since their initial moments as strangers. She's gone back to hunting deer now, he thought, and slogging through the tundra. After peeking out of concealment for a self-confident moment, she had scurried back in.

With Carol gone, he sat at his desk with his manuscript before him. Eighteen pages. His unfocussed stare, his freshly washed body and spent force seemed to clarify and elevate him. He laid his palm on the pile of paper, thinking, I have dipped my toe over sanity's edge, so this had better be good. He rubbed his eyes and began to read his story when from far down below he heard the front door slam shut. Lena was home. Home with her face deeply wrinkled like a desiccated overripe pepper, her mouth drawn down, her breasts flat, the hateful brown nicotine smell on her breath. He was getting angry again, filling up with hate for her stubborn self-destruction.

Turning to his story, reading and rereading it, he felt a terrible amazement that its sweet flood of sympathy and love for her was thriving in him even now, almost as though a very young and unmarked man had written it, a man imprisoned inside him, a free-singing poet whose spirit was as real and convincing as the waves of the sea. What if he tried to turn the story into a kind of paean to her as she once had been—would she recognize herself and be reconciled? As he read, he saw how perfectly beautiful and poetic she still was in some buried center of his mind, and remembered how merely waking with her in the mornings had once filled him with happiness and purpose. Looking up from the manuscript to stare out across the barren rooftops, he felt a pang for Carol, whose brutally young presence was still vibrating in the room, and he wanted her to return maybe one more time so that he could write on her tight skin again and perhaps dredge up some other innocent thing that might be shivering in the darkness inside him, some remnant of love so terrified of coming out that it seemed to have disappeared—taking with it his art.

THE TURPENTINE
STILL

Part 1

That winter in the early fifties was unusually cold in New York, or at least seemed so to Levin. Unless at thirty-nine he had prematurely aged, an idea he secretly rather liked. For the first time in his life he really longed to get away to the sun, so when Jimmy P. returned all tanned from Haiti he listened with more than sociological interest to his rapturous report of a new democratic wind blowing through the country. Levin, rather ahead of his time, had come to doubt that politics ever really changed human behavior for the better, and apart from his business, had turned his mind to his music and a few exemplary books. But even in his more political past he had never quite trusted Jimmy's enthusiasms, although he felt warmed by Jimmy's naïve respect. A former Colgate wrestler with a flattened nose and sloping shoulders and a lisp, Jimmy was a sentimental Communist who idolized talented people, some of whom he represented as a publicity man, as well as Stalin and any individual who showed signs of flaunting whatever respectable rule happened to be in play at the moment. Rebellion to Jimmy was poetic. The day of his seventh birthday his heroic father had kissed the top of his head and left to join a revolution in

Bolivia, and he never really returned except for some unexpected visits lasting a couple of weeks until he disappeared forever. But a fossilized shred of expectancy of the man's
reappearance may still have lurked in Jimmy's mind, feeding
his idolatrous bent. What he admired in Mark Levin was his
courage in having quit his job at the *Tribune* to take over his father's boring leather business rather than editorialize with the
new anti-Russian bellicosity demanded of him. The truth, however, was that Levin's mind was on Marcel Proust. During the
past year or so Proust's books had crowded very nearly everything else out of his thoughts except for his music, his cher-
ished combative wife Adele, and a comforting hypochondria.

Haiti, for Levin and Adele, was the dark side of the moon.
What they knew of the place had been gleaned from their den-
tist's *National Geographics* and the Carnival photos of wild-
looking women, some strikingly beautiful, dancing in the
streets, and Voodoo. But according to Jimmy, an inexplicably
sophisticated outbreak of remarkable painting and writing was
taking place now, exploding like a suppressed force of nature
in a country ruled for generations by knife and gun. Jimmy's old
friend, former *New York Post* columnist Lilly O'Dwyer, would
be eager to welcome the Levins; she had moved down there to
live with her expatriate mother and knew everybody, especially
the new young painters and intellectuals who were trying to
insinuate leftist democratic reforms before being murdered or
run out of the country. In the last election, the opposition can-
didate, his wife, and their four children had been hatcheted to
death in their street-level parlor by parties unknown.

The Levins were eager to go. Their last winter vacation—an

endless five days on a Caribbean beach—had sworn them off such brainless self-indulgence, but this promised to be different. The Levins were serious people; in an era before foreign films were shown in New York, they joined a society devoted to showing them in living rooms, and Mark especially was full of passion about the French and Italians. He and his wife were both accomplished classical pianists and in fact had first met at their piano teacher's home, she arriving for her lesson as he was leaving, and were immediately drawn to each other's unusual height. Mark was six four, Adele an even six feet; their pairing had normalized what they had borne as a kind of deformation, even if it still sprinkled a defensive irony over their conversations. Mark would say, "I've finally found a girl into whose eyes I can look without sitting down."

"Yes," she would add, "and one of these days he's going to decide to look at me."

Adele's face under her bangs and short-cropped hair had an almost Oriental cast, her black eyes and wide cheekbones squinching up her gaze, and Mark had a long, horsey face and dense kinky hair and a shyly reluctant laugh, except for the days when, muttering in despair, he once again believed that his stomach had tragically dropped or that his heart had shifted slightly toward the center of his chest. Still, beneath a guarded irony they could be naïve enough to be swept up, at least at a discreet distance, in one or another idealistic scheme for social improvement. Eating lunch in his Long Island City office, he read *The New Republic* with an occasional dutiful glance at *The New Masses* and drank his milk sometimes coursing over *Remembrance of Things Past* in the French he loved only a little less than his music. They flew to Port-au-Prince in the roaring cabin of a Pan American Constellation, both of them fending off the premonition that the trip was fated to be one more bead on the string of their mistakes.

The O'Dwyer house, finished the year before, hung like a rambling concrete nest over Port-au-Prince's harbor. Designed by Mrs. Pat O'Dwyer and son-in-law, Vincent Breede, in her version of the Frank Lloyd Wright spirit, the house induced breezes to blow freely through its wide rooms and windows. Mrs. Pat was at the moment in deep concentration in a poker game with Episcopal Bishop Tunnel, Commander Banz of the United States heavy cruiser anchored in mid-harbor, and the Chief of Police, Henri Ladrun. Around them a vast Oriental carpet spread out to white walls covered with a Klee, a Léger, and a half dozen brightly colored Haitian paintings, the latter testimony to Mrs. Pat's taste and acumen, their prices having skyrocketed since she had bought them well before Haitian painters had begun to sell. She had quickly taken a liking to Adele this evening, sharing anger at right-wing Congressmen and Republicans in general for instigating the current hunt for Reds in government, a specious slandering of liberal New Dealers in her view, and for being the party of the infamous Senator McCarthy.

Jimmy P. had primed the Levins about Mrs. Pat before they left New York. Starting out as a social worker in Providence, Rhode Island, she had early on concluded that what her mainly Catholic clients needed most were condoms, which at the time were under-the-counter items where they weren't illegal. Carrying boxes of them up from New York where she bought them on consignment, she graduated into becoming a distributor and finally opened a plant to manufacture them, ultimately acquiring great wealth. On vacation in Haiti, she perceived an even greater need for her product here and started another factory, this time donating the largest part of the production to nonprofit organizations. Nearing eighty now, handsome as ever with flowing silver hair and a blue-eyed gaze as placid as a pond, Mrs. Pat had a life that consisted of trying to make people get to the point. Impatience had converted her from Catholicism to the Christian Science that she interpreted as a faith in self-reliance, thus expressing her personal entrepreneurship and, in its larger application, her goal of a socialist, caring society.

Stretched out on a chaise near the card table reading her three-day-old *Times,* her daughter, Lilly said, "Jean Cours saw Charles Lebaye on the street yesterday." Defeated in her battle with weight, Lilly wore flowing white gowns and negligees. Locally made tin bracelets tinkled on her arms. Her eye had caught the entry of her eleven-year-old Peter, child of her first marriage to an alcoholic New York theatre critic, and she couldn't help thinking he had his father's dreaded black Irish moodiness and handsome elegance. Peter, in dirty tan shorts and barefoot, was stuffing his mouth with cherries out of a fruit bowl and not deigning to acknowledge her greeting, taunting her, she thought, for depriving him of his father.

Mrs. Pat hardly glanced up from her hand. "Saw Lebaye the Commissioner?"

"Yes."

"But I thought he died a week or so ago."

"He did." The card game stopped. Vincent and Levin came in from the balcony to hear, and all the players turned to Lilly. "Cours saw him in his casket and attended the burial."

"How could he know it was Lebaye?"

"He's known him all his life. He says he went up to him on the street but he walked right past him. He's been turned into a zombie, he says."

"What's a zombie?" Adele asked, turning to Vincent, who as a black Jamaican was likely to know.

Vincent said, "A kind of slave. They claim to resurrect a dead person and draw out his spirit so he does whatever the capturer wants."

"But what is it really?" Levin asked, towering over the card table and feeling his carotid artery with his index finger to test his pulse.

"I don't know, I think they possibly drug the victim and pretend to bury him. . . ."

"Cours swears he saw him going into the ground," Lilly said.

"He may have seen a casket going in, dear, but . . ." Vincent said.

"Some very strange things do happen," the bishop interrupted. All turned to him as the most experienced with Haitians, having converted a few as well as promoting the new painting and writing in the country. The whitewashed interior of his large church was covered with fresh pictures. With his melon-shaped pink face he had a pleasantly incompetent air, but he had sheltered revolutionaries and duped men with guns looking for them. "I'm not at all sure drugs are involved," he said. "They have a way of getting at the core of things, you know. I mean it's more like a kind of deep hypnotism that gets them to the center of a person."

"But they couldn't have actually buried the man," Commander Banz said, "he'd have suffocated." Black-haired, with a flawless profile, his white naval uniform with its standup collar perfectly fitted around his neck, he looked more the militant priest than the overweight bishop. Patriotically disagreeing with everything Mrs. Pat believed about U.S. imperial skulduggery, Banz found her a superior woman, an elegant mystery waiting to be solved. In any case, this house was the only place on the whole island where he felt welcome.

"Unless they had a way of slowing down his metabolism," Vincent said, "but I don't believe any of it."

Chief Ladrun, a short two-hundred-and-ninety-pounder whose belly seemed to start below his chin, was the only Haitian in the room. With a contented laugh he said, "It's all nonsense. Lots of people resemble one another. Voodoo is a religion like all the others, except there is more magic of course. But recall the loaves and fishes and the walking on water."

The conversation turned to magic, the game picked up again, and Lilly went back to her paper. Vincent and Levin returned to the balcony, where they sat side by side facing the harbor. Vincent, the only black man Levin had had the chance to talk to since his basket-shooting afternoons at college, was impressive to Levin. He knew by now that starting out as a poor, powerfully built Jamaican, Vincent held degrees from Oxford and a Swedish university and was in charge of the UN agency for reforestation of the Caribbean area. And Levin felt

rather pleased by Vincent's open interest in him and his fascination with Proust.

"Is Voodoo serious?" Levin asked.

"Well, you know the saying—Haiti is ninety percent Catholic and a hundred percent Voodoo. My personal view is that it's
more of a nuisance than anything else, but I think all religion
at bottom is a means of social control, so I can't take its spiri-
tual side too seriously. This country needs scientists and clear
thinkers, not magicians. But I suppose like anything else it has
its good uses. In fact, I've used it myself." He tended to excuse
any assertion with a chuckle.

He had arranged for a planting, he explained, of several
thousand fast-growing trees, charcoal being the basic fuel here.
Hardly a year later the small seedlings had all been cut down
and carted off for burning. "After I finished being outraged," he
said, "I happened to be at my barber's one day and he suggested I look up the local *houngan,* who might help. I found the
guy; for a donation he arranged a ceremony to make the planting area sacred. A big crowd showed up to watch the planting,
and nobody bothered the sacred trees for three years until they
were properly harvested. I must say I hated the idea but it did
work." After a moment's silence he asked, "Why are you interested in Haiti?"

"I didn't know I was," Levin said, "but there's some kind
of atmospheric attraction, a kind of secrecy, maybe. I really
don't know."

He looked at the black man's face in the glow of yellow light
from the living room, and with the dark waters of the harbor
beyond him and the sparse lights of the impoverished city be-

low, the strangeness of his being here struck him, and with it an apprehension, like finding himself over his head swimming in the sea. He enjoyed his safety but longed for the risks of an artist rather than the waste of his daily wrangle with business. "I hop along solidly on one foot, the other suspended over a cliff," he once said to Adele after they had finished a Schubert duet that had moved him almost to tears.

"Would you and your wife like to see more of the country? I have to go up into the pine forest tomorrow." Vincent faced him, a thick-shouldered man in his thirties, infinitely confident and at ease in this black country.

Eager to see into this strange place, Levin instantly agreed, surprised by the shock of anticipation he had almost forgotten was still alive in him. Proust's beloved face flashed across his mind, *like a dead flower,* he thought.

Part 2

When Adele saw the tiny Austin in the driveway of the Gustafson Hotel she begged off, preferring to spend the day sightseeing in town rather than sitting sideways for hours in its backseat. Actually, she planned to wander around the hotel for a while; its unremodeled French colonial style reminded her of a sunken relic. Through its tall, gauzy curtained windows she could imagine Joseph Conrad passing by or sitting in one of the lobby's enormous rattan chairs, and there must be some shops that Mark would have no patience for. She waved happily at the departing little car.

As the Austin moved past her, the early sun was still low enough to flood her amused face under her wide-brimmed, black straw hat; it was a soft light that seemed to elevate and suspend her in space, and Levin reprimanded himself for not making love to her more often. What was it now, a week? Maybe longer. A quiet alarm sounded in him. Tossing their ironies and sage observations back and forth was no substitute for horned clashes such as he had in business, and he resolved to begin trying to get to know Adele again. Seven years into their marriage, and they had lost a lot of curiosity. He had to stop hiding himself. He had to start listening again.

Vincent threaded the car down the town's main streets and around telephone poles that drooped broken wires, some of them planted like distracted afterthoughts in the middle of streets or a few feet from a curb, some on the sidewalks. Overhanging second stories shaded the interiors of shops open to the street, in most of which men seemed to be repairing pots, car fenders, broken furniture. An enormous store on one corner sold tires, stoves, refrigerators, meat, fish, dresses, boots, kerosene, gas. The bank's windows were spotless, and through them Levin saw young women cashiers in starched white blouses working solemnly at what were no doubt the best jobs in town. A couple of neatly dressed, unsmiling businessmen stood on the sidewalk, hands clasped in a dignified morning handshake. There was still time for everything here.

Vincent tugged at the steering wheel around turns. "English steering," he laughed, "tight but accurate. This thing is built to improve character—I think I've pushed it more than I've driven it. If there's a rumor of a distant mist the thing won't start."

The town thinned out and the surprisingly good blacktop road wound through clusters of shacks and tiny gardens, almost always worked by a woman while the man sat nearby talking to her or a friend. "The men don't seem to do anything much," Levin observed.

"Africa," Vincent said. "The man hunted and the woman did the house and the planting. Of course, there's nothing here left to hunt. Some of them do work hard, but they need education. It's desperate. This country is waiting to start existing."

"What can they export?" Levin asked. Every cluster of shacks seemed to have a hand-lettered sign advertising *reparations pneu.* "Aside from repairs?"

"Bauxite. The ore to make aluminum. There used to be gold. Not much, but it's long gone."

Levin found himself trying to imagine improving things. "And what could they do with more education? Aside from emigrating?"

"Get a decent government, to start with. That would be a great thing." Vincent's grave intensity deepened his voice. He had suddenly stopped kidding; Levin was surprised. It reminded him of his own frantic political arguments in college, so long ago.

The car had been climbing for half an hour past deepening pine growth, and the air smelled cool and fresh now. "Who owns all this?"

"The State. But the politicians are stealing it away."

"How?"

"Fiddling the books."

"Is it being replanted?"

"No. That's what I'm trying to get done. It's doomed, the whole forest, but public office is a license to steal," Vincent said.

Levin's body tightened with a kind of combativeness that he instantly recognized as absurd—it wasn't his forest, and anyway, what could he do about it?

A lone woman suddenly appeared out of the forest leading a stubborn goat by a rope. Her long body moved like an effortless dream figure that hardly touched the earth, and the tail of a long crimson bandanna was wound around her head and streamed over her breast like a wound. She held out one gracefully waving arm for balance, like a dancer.

"A lot of them are very beautiful," Levin said.

"That's the pity of it, yes."

The road leveled out and, in a clearing, Levin saw an Alpine-style log cabin with a steeply pitched roof and deep eaves, here where it never snowed.

"I have to pay respects to the manager," Vincent said as he got out and disappeared into the building. Levin got out of the car and stretched, going up on his toes. The silence was like a soft stroke on his flesh. At that moment, his standing on this particular spot on the earth was somehow miraculous. What was he doing here? In the car Vincent had mentioned a man he would have to talk to today. He had laughed about the fellow, a onetime Madison Avenue ad executive who had gone native up here. He had said more but the noise from the transmission had garbled it. Now he emerged from the building, laughing along with a black man who hung back and was waving goodbye.

"One of the lesser crooks," Vincent said as he drove away. In a few minutes, they were off the road altogether, following an earthen trail through the woods. Trees were much larger here, harder to get at and fell than the ones at the periphery of the forest. Presently they came to a simple log bungalow. Newspaper was stuffed into a broken window and a spavined red Ford pickup sat alongside it. Metal parts of some machine were scattered over the weedy clearing, along with bald tires, a large awning, window frames, a rusted hand pump, and a forlorn outhouse leaning against a tree. Everything seemed to be leaning. The porch steps were warped. A clothesline stretched between two trees with a single bra hanging from it. Vincent turned off the engine but remained behind the wheel. His chuckling ironies had disappeared, and Levin thought he saw some tension around his eyes.

"Who's this again? I didn't quite catch . . ."

"Douglas. It's a ticklish problem," he said, for the first time looking uncertain. "I shouldn't have allowed myself to get into it, but at the time I didn't think he'd ever get this far."

"You've lost me. What are you talking about?" Vincent had evidently forgotten that not everyone was up on this situation.

He settled back in his seat, his eyes on the house with only an occasional glance toward Levin. "I like the man but he's very odd. Good-hearted, you know, but . . . well, I guess you could call him silly. Quit an important job a couple of years ago with BBD&O on Madison Avenue to cruise around with his family on a surplus Navy boat, showing films to people on the various islands." Now he laughed, but the tension stayed in his face. "Actually thought he could make a living selling tickets to the natives! And of course there weren't enough customers with a quarter in their pockets, not in the Caribbean. So he arrived here, probably looking for something he could do with his boat, I think. And—God knows where the idea came from, I've never understood that part of it—but I think it was when he saw this gigantic tank near the dock he'd tied up at. It may have come off some large wreck. It could hold, I don't know, probably a few thousand gallons. And there it lay doing nothing. He hung around, living on the boat with his family, filling himself up with frustration about the tank."

"Because it wasn't doing anything."

"Of course! Yes!" He laughed again. "We're all forever saving Haiti. You seem to have some of that feeling yourself."

"Well, not really, although I guess I can understand it. Maybe it's the people; they seem so . . ."

"Sweet, yes. And so full of imag*ination,*" he gave the word a celebratory Jamaican lilt. "Anyway, he heard of the forest and came up here one day, and the thought hit him that with all this pine he could harvest the resin for turpentine and set up a distillation process. Turpentine's a big thing in Haiti; they use it for everything from rheumatism to chest and sex problems and a dozen other things. So he had the tank and suddenly here was a terrific use for it." He burst out laughing, but the concern was still there in his eyes. "Not only have a use for the tank but help protect the forest, and create maybe a couple of dozen good jobs for people. It had a lot of different virtues, like turpentine itself."

He paused, still staring at the house. His lips had dried, and he wet them with his tongue. "I really didn't mean to, but I guess I inadvertently encouraged him. I was the only one around with some scientific background, although what he really needed was engineering advice. He had some friends at the ad agency send him literature about distillation technology, and he pumped me for the chemistry I barely remembered, and he was off. First thing, he'd learned that the tank had to lie at a specific angle—I've forgotten exactly what degree that was—but he got hold of some surveyor's stuff and went about up here until he'd found a grade with precisely the incline he needed, and hired a couple of men to set up concrete pillows to support the tank. Of course the thing was far too large to be trucked up here so I unfortunately found him a welder I knew down in the port, and he had the thing cut into sections, brought it up piece by piece in his pickup and welded it back into shape again. The whole thing was so absurd that I . . ." He broke off, dead serious now. "I guess I feel somewhat responsible, although I tried to discourage him. Even so . . ." He paused again, confused. "I don't know, maybe I encouraged him too, in the sense that I was glad that *somebody* was enthusiastic about this country's possibilities. I simply—I don't know, I think I should have taken it more seriously. The danger, I mean."

"How long has he been at this?"

"It must be at least eight months, maybe a year. It's crazy—if you need a nail there's nothing between here and the port, so he or his wife had to be running up and down the mountain to fetch the least little thing."

"But what's worrying you? It all seems harmless enough," Levin said.

"He's ready to light the fire."

"And?"

"That tank will fill with vapor. He's got some kind of relief valve on the top, but Christ, I don't know if it's the right one; it's just some damned thing he picked up in the port. Valves like this have different capacities and I know nothing about them, any more than he does." A nervous high-pitched laugh escaped him now: "The steam pressure has to be around a hundred seventy pounds per square inch and all his equipment is secondhand or improvised. That's a lot of pressure for equipment that's been rewelded, with welds on top of welds, and fiddled around with. God knows, he could blow off the top of this mountain or set fire to the forest and kill himself in the bargain!"

"When is this supposed to happen?"

"Today."

"You'd better steal his matches and get us the hell out of here." Both men burst out laughing. "What *are* you going to do?"

"Well, I'm certainly going to try to talk him out of it. He's got to get some professional engineering advice."

"You'd think he'd have done that a long time ago."

Suddenly, out of the corner of his eye, Levin saw a face looking in at his window, but the instant he turned it was gone. It had seemed the face of a child.

"That's Catty," Vincent said, slipping out of his seat. As they walked up to the house he continued, "There's also Richard, who's seven, I think, and she's about nine. Listen." He halted, facing Levin. "I wish you'd ask him where the kids go to school. Because I don't think they have in all the time they've been up here, they're just running wild with the local kids. He won't listen to me, thinks I'm one of these over-conventional niggers. Could you do that?"

A woman appeared on the narrow porch, her arm in a white sling. "Vincent! How nice!" With a careful glance down at a broken step, she hurried across the weeds to them with her good hand extended like a hostess at some elegant lunch. Denise was small and vivacious, in her mid-forties. A wild distraction flared in her eager eyes, and her fair hair was twisted and knotted, probably, Levin thought, because she couldn't wash it with one hand. She never ceased to smile, but "Please rescue" was like a lit sign hanging over her head.

"What happened?" Vincent asked, indicating the sling.

"Oh Vincent," she began, and grasped his upper arm for more than physical support, a wan look on her face now. "I was unloading one of the fifty-five-gallon drums, and it slipped and hit me. I'm healing but it was awful for a while, the truck wouldn't start and the children were off somewhere and Douglas was over at the tanks. So I had to walk holding it together. . . ."

Vincent, Levin saw, was clearly her savior, her one hope of escaping whatever it was that had an obviously upper-class woman grappling fifty-five-gallon drums. She must have felt she was dreaming until it cracked her bone. "Come, come inside, he'll be so glad to see you." Levin was only now introduced as they entered the house, but she hardly glanced at him, her whole attention fixed on Vincent.

The room they entered had a dank smell. In one wall was an immense fireplace made of round boulders with a mantel on which four or five tattered books stood. There were no chairs or tables, only a few scattered wooden boxes, on one of which lay the unwashed dishes of a recent meal. A dusty filigreed pump organ stood against one wall, and on one of the boxes sat a perspiring man in work boots, torn jeans and T-shirt, and an oil-stained Yankees cap, studying blueprints spread out on his lap and around the floor, his tongue sticking out between his lips. One lens of his small wire-rimmed glasses was cracked, and the misshapen frame had a temple piece missing, replaced by a white string looped around his ear. Several days' growth of beard had been shaved in spots, as though absentmindedly, leaving graying tufts. There was a darkness in the room despite the sunny day; the windows set high in the walls under the broad eaves of the roof seemed to admit shadow rather than light.

"Vincent's here, darling!" the woman fairly shrieked as they entered.

It took Douglas a good half minute to come out of his rapt concentration. Then he sprang up and threw his arms around Vincent, still clutching the blueprint, and quickly shook hands with Levin without looking at him. His oil-stained hand was rough as sandpaper. Douglas was tall and politely stooped, and Levin recognized the Ivy League as soon as he began to speak.

"Son of a gun, where've you been, I've been waiting for you all week!" Three children—two white, one black—flicked past the screen door and disappeared as quick as deer.

"Would you like a tea before we go?" he asked, his arm lingering on Vincent's shoulder, a comradely gesture from which Vincent seemed to shrink. "I think we have tea, don't we, darling?" He looked around for his wife but she had vanished, and he called toward the back of the house, "Is there tea, darling?"

When no answer came back Vincent suggested, "Why don't we sit down for a minute first, Doug?"

"Of course, yes, sorry." Douglas leaped up and pulled another box over, his gait rocking, bear-like. At this point Vincent, aware that Douglas had not really taken in Levin's presence, introduced him again; Douglas turned to him with surprise, as though he had dropped through the ceiling. "Yes! Very nice to meet you. Sorry for the accommodations," he chuckled and turned back to Vincent, who had sat down facing him. His wife reappeared and sat on a box, her good hand resting protectively on the cast. She had managed to brush out her hair and change into fresh jeans and a peach blouse which sketched out her breasts, and this attempt at renewal touched Levin. He sensed in her high nervousness the culmination of some struggle which had determined her to enlist Vincent on her side.

But Douglas seemed oblivious. "I've been ready to go since last weekend." Despite his smile a touch of complaint was in his tone. "What's happened? Where have you been?"

Vincent set himself for a second or two and began, "I've been busy. But I really have to remind you, Doug, that I've never set myself up as . . . I mean I don't feel I have a particular responsibility for this."

"Of course not. I never expected that. But I did think you had an *interest*."

"I do, but I may as well be candid with you, Doug, I don't really feel confident in the whole process. As far as I can understand it anyway. As I told you last time I was here—I've asked around concerning the type of tree we have up here—"

"I'm aware of that," Douglas interrupted.

"*Pinus sylvestris* is the right kind—"

"Well, it's the best kind, yes, but there's plenty of resin in these too."

"Doug, I have to ask you to listen to me." Vincent's voice had risen and the hard core in it struck Levin for the first time. Douglas kept quiet but the effort showed. "They apparently call for a live steam temperature of around a hundred degrees centigrade in the melter—"

"Eighty-five to a hundred."

"Apparently that depends on the quality of the resin, and the kind you have here is poor. My point, Doug, is this: you've got rewelded tanks, and I've noticed some rust—"

"That's entirely superficial."

"But how sure are you of that? The pressure can go to 150 psi and the temperature to 170. All I'm trying to tell you, Doug, is that—"

"The thing is perfectly safe!" Douglas stood up. "Where did you get your information?"

"I talked to Commander Banz."

"Off that *battleship*? What could he possibly know about turpentine?"

"He comes from Alabama. They do a lot of it there and his family was involved—"

"Gawwd!" Douglas turned his face toward a deaf heaven, "a *Navy guy* spouting off about turpentine!" He tramped around snapping his cap on his thigh like a thwarted boy. "I've been in command, Vincent, you know that. Sixteen months on a fucking tin can destroyer, and I'm here to tell you that no Navy guy knows piss about turpentine. He's thinking of his goddamn boilers, which are a whole different story."

Levin had a hard time keeping a serious look on his face. But a certain genuineness nevertheless reached him in Douglas's anguish, an authentic outcry such as he had never met with, at least not in a cultivated man. Neither he nor anyone he knew, he suddenly realized, had ever cared this much and this openly. But all for the sake of turpentine? Levin doubted that money lay behind it all—turpentine was too inexpensive, he reasoned. What was it then?

"Darling, you really need to at least listen to Vincent," Denise said.

"Well, are you proposing something?" Douglas asked.

Vincent paused for a moment, then spoke: "I have nothing but respect, Doug, for what you've been trying to accomplish up here—"

"God's sake, Vince, you'd have jobs up here, you'd have self-respect for once, there'd be people working and preventing all this theft. This country is *dying*, Vincent!"

His eyes were filled with pain, the sight of which repelled Levin, who promptly damned himself for insensitivity. A kind of undirected disgust lingered around the edges of his mind as the two men and Denise agreed to drive over to the still and have a look at things. Levin found it incredible that despite all the uncertainty Douglas was apparently still determined to start up the process.

Vincent and Levin rode in the Austin, with Douglas and Denise following in the pickup. Vincent's temper had surfaced and he kept plunging the car ahead and braking. "This is really not my business, you know." For some reason he was apologizing to Levin, who himself felt some unnamable responsibility, why and for what he could not begin to explain to himself.

"He's put together a lot of junk. It's junk! I'm certainly not going to hang around if he lights it up."

"What about their kids?"

"I don't know. I just don't know."

Levin saw steel cups on some of the tree trunks, and Vincent explained they caught the resin flowing from cuts in the cambium layer above them. The air here was almost cold, like Northern Europe. Odd that a few miles down the mountain was the warm sea. "Of course, they're the wrong kind of pine. But don't ask me why. This is not my expertise."

"What is it with him?" Levin asked. "Vanity? I mean he can't be expecting to make a lot of money for himself, or can he?"

"Possibly, if he had a number of stills, but he only has this one. I'm not sure it's vanity, though. He does love the country, although I think she's just about had it here."

"I forgot to ask him about the children's schooling."

"Doesn't matter, I know what he'd answer: he'll point to those books on the mantel. A history of the world as of 1925 or something, a chemistry textbook from around 1910, a Kipling collection of stories, and one other I can't recall . . . oh yes, a world atlas. Which still has India colored British pink."

"What about her? Isn't she concerned?"

"You saw his stubbornness." He paused for a moment. "He's in love, you see."

"With?"

"I don't know how to put it. With the idea, maybe. Of . . ." He struggled for the word, then seemed to give up. "You see, he was after German subs in the area during the war and fell in love. With the sun and that marvelous sea. That was before the tourists, of course, or anything like a technological civilization. There were horse carriages in the port, and the beaches were like virgins, he said to me once. It was all terribly poor but hadn't got spoiled yet. So he dreamed about living down here and cooked up this idea of showing movies on that boat. I sometimes wonder if it's really very simple—he just wanted to *start* something. We all do, I guess, but for some people it's absolutely necessary. To be the germ of something, the inventor, the one who begins it. I say that because he had a very good spot in New York and the house in Greenwich, the whole pot. But he wasn't *starting* anything. In a way he was looking for a fight, I guess." He laughed, shook his head. "And this is the place, if that's what you want."

"He wants to do good, you think?"

"Oh yes, he wants that, but I've come to think that's maybe not the main thing."

"To kind of invent himself. To create something."

"I think so."

Levin stared at the dirt path ahead, the holes and boulders. He had no children and had come to believe that his low sperm count was lucky. He just wasn't a father, certainly not now that he was approaching forty. For one thing he had all the time he wanted for piano, and Adele did too. No regrets about that. Or would she agree? Bumping along in the tiny car, his knees up to the dashboard, he wondered whether Adele was really as content with childlessness as she made out. He thought of painful hints, gestures, a tear he had once noticed in her eye when looking into the cradle of a friend's infant son. He inwardly groaned at these memories. What was he doing in Haiti, in this nonsensical place where he understood nothing? He felt bereft, abandoned, and suddenly he wondered whether Adele loved him, even whether her quick decision to stay in town today had some other purpose. A ridiculous thought—she would never betray him. But there it was. And instantly the idea effloresced into bloom: she had waited till the last minute when it would be too late for him to cancel the trip, leaving her free to move into that unknowable city, a white woman alone. . . .

They were on the highway for no more than half a mile when Vincent turned off again onto a path, and they came on it suddenly in a clearing: the black tank lay up against the mountain at an angle like a resting monster, connected by a tangle of piping to several smaller tanks placed at various heights beside and above it. A massive pile of pine logs twice a man's height stood nearby, as well as a cement mixer, barrels, steel drums, sleeping dogs, and half-a-dozen men moving about drinking water, laughing together or staring into space.

Levin got out of the car as Denise approached. Vincent walked over to the tanks with Douglas, who was explaining something. Denise said in a rather conspiratorial hush, "We have an organ, you know."

"Yes, I noticed it."

"Perhaps you could play for us."

"Oh. Well . . ." How did she know he played? Unanswered

questions were exhausting him. He wasn't even sure he'd told Vincent that he and Adele played, and then Vincent's voice turned him toward the tanks.

"You're just going to have to listen to me, Douglas!" he was yelling. And Douglas was literally writhing as he tried to interrupt his friend, twisting his head toward the sky and stamping one foot. "I know what this means to you, Douglas, but it's all a mistake, you can't possibly start this up without a professional inspection."

"You—"

"No!" Vincent yelled, a pleading tone in his voice, "I'm not competent, I've told you a hundred times, and I will not be held responsible—"

"But the pressures aren't—"

"I don't know that and you don't either! I ask you to wait! Just wait, for God's sake, until you can find someone who—"

"I can't wait," Douglas said quietly.

It would always strike Levin that at this instant, when Douglas had stopped shouting and became quiet, a very distant chain saw went silent. As though the whole world was listening in on this.

"Why can't you wait?" Vincent asked, curiosity overtaking his anger.

"I'm ill," Douglas said.

"What do you mean?"

"I have a cancer."

Vincent instinctively reached out and grasped his friend's wrist. The workers were all beyond earshot at the moment, standing around waiting for Douglas's orders. "I must see it working before I go," Douglas said.

"Yes," Vincent agreed. Denise had gone over to her husband and was clasping his arm. Levin saw how in love they were, she so unfitted for this life, sacrificing even her children's education so Douglas could live out his necessary fantasy. "I'm returning to the port this afternoon. Let me make some calls," Vincent said. "I'm sure I can get someone, if necessary, from our Miami office. There must be people there who'd know whom to bring down, somebody who could give us an expert opinion." The *us* seemed to melt Douglas's stiff defensive posture; at last they were in this together, at least to an extent that validated the thing, making it real. Douglas gripped Vincent's neck and drew him close; Denise stretched forward and kissed Vincent's cheek. The relief playing over Vincent's face astonished Levin, who felt grateful that nothing terrible had exploded between the two friends, but unlike Vincent, he wasn't quite taken in by the outbreak of hopefulness on all sides. After all, nothing about the tanks or the process had been resolved; an air of doom still hung undisturbed over the project. Nothing had really happened except that the three of them had been joined in some passion of mutual reconciliation.

Back at the bungalow, Douglas and Denise stood waving goodbye as Vincent backed the car to make the turn onto the path. They were strikingly happy, Levin thought, at peace, where only a couple of hours ago tensions were flying about all over the place. The car negotiated the holes and boulders. Levin wondered what he had missed that would explain why everything had changed, especially in Vincent. And all he could come up with was the obvious—that Vincent had at long last accepted, however inadvertently, if not a responsibility for the project then a kind of participation in it by offering to bring in expertise from abroad. To that extent he had identified himself with Douglas's dream.

"Will you be calling Miami?" Levin asked, unable to strip the ironical coating from his voice.

Vincent glanced at him. "Certainly. Why do you ask?" He seemed almost offended by Levin's tone.

"Just that . . ." Levin broke off. The whole event was so tangled in his mind that he didn't know where to grasp one of its threads. "You suddenly seemed to, I don't know, believe in the process. I'd had the idea you didn't at all."

"I don't think I said I didn't believe in it, but I still don't know if I do or don't. I was just glad he showed a willingness to put off firing the thing up."

"I see," Levin said.

They fell silent. In other words, Levin reasoned, for the sake of peace Vincent was pretending to believe in the reality of the process while Douglas was similarly pretending that someone beside himself was sharing responsibility for what could turn out a catastrophe. The two of them were creating a kind of fantasy of shared belief. Levin felt a certain pleasure rising in himself, the pleasure of clarity, and his mind inevitably turned to Proust. But now he saw the great author differently; Proust, he said to himself, was also a pretender. He pretended to an absolute accuracy in describing towns, streets, smells, people, but after all he was describing nothing but his fantasy.

They'd stayed longer on the mountain than Levin realized. They lunched late by the roadside on sandwiches Vincent had brought, and by the time they reached the lower edges of the forest, it was dark. Levin had taken over the wheel to relieve Vincent, and as they chatted, Levin had to strain to make out the winding, tilted road. The headlights, he realized, were penetrating the darkness less and less, until abruptly they went out and the engine died. He coasted over to the side of the road and kicked the starter button on the floor, with no result. "The battery's died," he said. Vincent found a flashlight in the glove compartment, and they got out of the car and lifted the hood. Levin wiggled the battery cable and tried the starter again, but it was dead. The two men stood in the total dark, in the silence.

"What now?" Levin asked. "Are there people around, you suppose?"

"They're watching us right now."

"Where?" Levin turned toward the roadsides.

"Everywhere."

"Why?"

"Waiting to see what happens." Vincent laughed appreciatively.

"You mean they're actually sitting out there in the dark?"

"That's right." Vincent sat down on the front bumper and leaned forward.

Levin cocked his ears toward the dark roadsides. "Can't hear them."

"You won't." Vincent giggled.

"And what would you say their mood was?"

"Curious."

Levin sat on the bumper next to Vincent. He could hear his friend's breathing, but in the absence of any nightshine he could barely define his head. Even the sky was lightless. Could there be people out there watching from the dark? What were they thinking? Would they decide to rob us? Or were we like two performers, he wondered, whom they enjoyed watching from their theatre in the overgrowth?

"Suppose we let her coast down? We might find a village, don't you think?"

"Ssh."

Levin listened, and soon registered the noise of a distant motor. Both men stood and looked toward the sound, toward the mountaintop where they had come from. Headlights were moving up there in the remote distance, and presently the truck appeared out of the night, an open flatbed packed with a crowd of people standing in the back. Vincent and Levin waved down the truck, and Vincent explained to the driver in Creole that their battery had quit. The driver opened the door and hopped down. He was young and trim and spoke surprisingly good English. "I think there may be a helpful thing here," he said as he walked to the back of the truck, where he lowered the tail-gate and shouted at the passengers to jump down. They poured off the truck without complaint. This was interesting for them. The driver leaped onto the bed and wrestled a tarpaulin off a dim pile of junk, speaking English all the while to impress *les blancs,* no doubt. "I believe is here something possibly . . . Ha!" His passengers burst into triumphant laughter with him as he danced off the truck bed and onto the road, where he handed a car battery to Levin. He hurried around to the truck's cabin and pulled some wrenches from under the seat, returned to the car, disconnected the battery, dropped the fresh one in, and clamped the cables. Levin squirmed into the car, turned the key, and the engine screamed to life and the headlights came on. He slid out and stood laughing along with the driver and the delighted Vincent.

"Let us pay you," he said, *"s'il vous plaît, permettez . . ."* He pulled out his wallet before the Austin's thankfully bright light beams.

"No-no," the driver said, holding up a palm. Then he spoke Creole to Vincent, who translated for Levin.

"He says we should simply return the battery to him in the next few days."

"But what's his address?" Levin asked. The driver was already climbing back into his truck.

"He just said to deliver it to one of the piers and ask for Joseph. Everybody knows him, he says."

"But which pier?"

"I have no idea," Vincent said as they got back into the car and started down the mountain.

Levin drove again, struggling now with amazement at their salvation, and beyond that, the trusting generosity of the driver. And even more impenetrable, the absence of surprise among the onlookers. Was it all simply another scene in the ongoing fantasy of their life, the sudden appearance of these *blancs* on the dark road, the appearance of this battery from under the tarpaulin? And how did the battery happen to be the right size for the Austin? And charged too?

"What do you suppose they made of all this?" Levin asked.

"Of what just happened?"

"Yes. Us suddenly being there, and him having the battery and all."

Vincent chuckled. "God knows. Probably that it was inevitable. Like everything else."

"They wouldn't think it odd that he didn't even want money from us? And trusted us to return the battery?"

"I doubt they'd think that very strange. Because in a way *everything* is so strange. This was just one more thing, I imagine. Most of what they live through can't be easily explained. It's all one wide flow of . . . whatever. Of time, I suppose." He fell silent except to indicate to Levin which turns to make through the streets. The town slept in darkness except for an occasional store, no more than a counter open to the street where people sat with soft drinks under orange lights, and children played at the edge of the dark, and a tethered donkey munched in a garbage pile.

Part 3

Thirty years passed. Thirty-three to be exact, as Mark Levin tried to be concerning time, "the last items in the inventory," as he called the passing hours and weeks. He was becoming obsessed by time, he told himself, not necessarily a good thing. Past seventy now, he was dropping tulip bulbs into holes he had punched in the small garden alongside the front door of his house. As Adele had had him do every fall so long ago, but this time he mused on whether he would see the flowers.

Everything now, as in some dreams, took forever to get done. He could hear the bumbling of waves in the near distance, felt a certain empty gratitude to the ocean for being there. The net bag empty, he covered the bulbs and stamped down the thin, sandy soil, took the digging tool to the garage and then went through his basement, up the stairs, and into his kitchen. The *Times* lay flat and virginal on the kitchen table, its news already outdated, and he wondered how many tons of *Times* he had read in his life and whether it had really mattered at all. He had seen the few good movies in surrounding towns and had no interest in television. The piano, which he hadn't touched in more than two months, remonstrated in its black silence. The light was dying fast outside on the sandy street. What to do with his evening and his night, aside from confronting self-pity and fending it off?

He had played less and less in the six years since Adele's death, gradually realizing that he had been playing for her approval, to a degree anyway, so that now it had lost some of its point. In any case he had finally agreed with himself that he would never reach the level he had once dreamed of, most certainly not alone. He was sitting at the kitchen counter where he had landed. There was no pain in his healthy body, but a practiced inner eye still supervised the beating of his heart and the positioning of his stomach. The question before him, he said to himself, was whether and why to get up and where to move to: the living room, his bedroom, the guest bedroom, or perhaps a walk in the empty street. He was a free man. But freedom without obligations, as it turned out, was something else. In such stasis his thoughts usually coursed over the ranks of the dead, of his small circle of friends, the last of whom he had recently survived, which left him wondering, with some flicker of pride, why he had been so chosen. But all the main questions were answerless.

Call Marie? Have a lover-like conversation with that dear person, only to remain unchanged by the dialing of her number, still more than twice her age, still and forever her mere friend? How stupid, how awful, to be the friend of the person one loves. "But if I made love to you," she'd said, "it would wall me off from someone else." Yes, someone of her generation. Time again. But the selfish bastard inside him howled before going agreeably silent. Better not to call her but to launch himself in some potent direction. He would be a free man until he fell to his knees.

And inevitably his mind, like a circling bird, landed on Adele, returning again and again to that worn but still glamorous vision of her from the Austin, standing before the Gustafson Hotel in her black straw, wide-brimmed hat, and the low morning sun holding her suspended in its yellowish light, fixed there, as it turned out, forever. How really beautiful she had looked then! How he wished to have shown her more of his love! But maybe he had; who knew? He got up, slipped into a light jacket that hung beside the front door and went into the street where the fall chill braced him.

The sun would be setting. He walked, his steps shorter than in time past, down the street and onto the beach, where he stood in the sand watching the sun slipping down to the horizon. Stiffly he lowered himself to sit on the cool sand. Soft waves made way for an occasional boomer. The beach was empty, as were most of the houses behind him now that October was looming. He thought of Douglas up there in the pine forest. Probably dead now. As poor Vincent was, after the local doctor had given him a mistaken injection of some kind the year after their short acquaintance.

Did anyone but him remember Vincent, he wondered? (And how could it have been thirty-three years ago when in his mind it was all so fresh?) Levin recalled now, staring at the waves, that Jimmy P., also dead, had once mentioned that the turpentine still had never been lit. Out of fear, Levin wondered, or for some business reason? Or had Jimmy gotten it wrong? But the main questions were always answerless.

He hated his loneliness, it was like a rank closet, a damp towel, loose shoes. Then why not offer marriage to the girl, make her his heir? But money had no meaning to her, and he had so little life to promise. But this endless string of days that threatened to unroll emptily before him was intolerable. Why not a trip to Haiti? Try to see how it all turned out. The thought, absurd as it seemed, quickened him, drove off his weariness. But who would he look up? Mrs. Pat was surely gone by now, and probably her daughter too. It was so odd that he alone might be carrying the pictures of these people in his mind. Except for him keeping them alive in the soft knot of tissue under his skull they might have no existence. And of them all, it was Douglas who returned most vividly to Levin, especially his Yankees cap and throaty voice; he could still hear him shouting, "This country is *dying,* Vincent!" The anguish in that man! The longing he must have had to . . . to what? What was he about?

Staring at the gray sea, the darkening sky, it was suddenly obvious to Levin that for Douglas the turpentine still must have been his work of art. Douglas was sacrificing himself, his career, his wife and children, to the creation of a vision of some beauty in his mind. Unlike me, Levin said to himself, or most people who never get to intercept that invisible beam which stirs them with its power to imagine something new. So what matters, he thought, was creation, the creation of what has not yet been. "And this I could never do," he said aloud, chilled now and tramping excitedly up the beach toward his house.

He stood still for a moment in the middle of his living room, struck by the question of whether—what was his name? The young son of—what was her name again? Yes, Lilly O'Dwyer. Peter! Yes, it was Peter. Could he still be there? He'd only be in his forties now. For the first time in memory, Levin felt life surging into him again. How glorious to be here, standing upright on the earth! To be free to think! To ride one's imaginings! He clapped his hands together and quickly found Adele's old address book in the drawer under the phone, and searched for their travel agent's number. Kendall Travel. Mrs. Kendall, yes. A very helpful woman.

"Kendall Travel, can I help you?"

She was alive! He recognized the voice. A wave of self-pity engulfed him as he realized he was going to Haiti, but alone. Then anguish all over again for his extinguished wife. And finally in the plane, wondering why he was doing this, going to a country that by all accounts had sunk into the abyss. What was behind it, he wondered? Could it be simply that he was an idle old man who needed something to do?

. . .

Peter O'Dwyer remembered him, an amazement to Levin who, however, had recognized him the moment he entered his small chaotic office on the pier. Two prefab metal windows looked out on the harbor with its half-sunk derelicts and a rusting freighter whose deck showed no sign of life. A dozen or so black workers were assembling and packing chairs in the corrugated steel warehouse through which Levin had passed to get here.

Peter was still the dark-skinned, barefoot child Levin recalled eating all the cherries on their first evening, only big now, almost his height, and powerfully built. There was something like meanness in his face, or just toughness, it was hard to tell, but he had remarkable water-gray eyes, like Weimaraner dogs.

"We make chairs for export, woven raffia," Peter replied to Levin's questions. "What brings you to Haiti? And how'd you know to find me?"

"The Gustafson manager."

"Right. Phil. What can I do for you?" There was something punished in his eyes.

"I won't take your time—"

"I remember you playing that night, a duet with your wife."

"I'd forgotten that."

"It was the first time anyone had gotten real music out of that piano."

"I hadn't thought of that in years. In fact, now that you mention it, I think it was a Schubert piece."

"I don't know that kind of music but it was really terrific." Peter's open admiration surprised Levin and helped launch him now. "You still playing?"

"No, not seriously. My wife died, for one thing."

"Oh, sorry. So what can I do for you?" he repeated, with some insistence this time.

"I've been wondering about that turpentine still up in the pine forest."

"The what?"

"The still that man Douglas put together up there. He was a good friend of Vincent's."

"Vincent died, you know."

"I heard. You didn't know Douglas?"

Peter shook his head.

Levin felt stymied; he'd assumed that in this small country with so few whites they would all know everything about one another. He felt alarm, and as he took in Peter's honest vacant look, the question crossed his mind whether (impossible, of course) Douglas had ever really existed.

Levin smiled, and making light of Douglas said, "He was kind of a whacko. Lived up there in the forest in a kind of wrecked bungalow with his family."

Peter shook his head. "Never heard of him. Did my mother know him?"

"I don't think so, but I'm pretty sure she knew *about* him. Is she . . . ?"

"She's gone. And grandma."

"Sorry to hear that."

"What'd you want with him?" Peter's interest at least had been captured, but confronted with the bald question Levin was at a loss. What *did* he want with Douglas? "I guess I . . . well, I'm curious whether he ever started up that still. Because Vincent was very concerned, you know, about an explosion." The explanation seemed ludicrous to Levin. An explosion thirty years ago had brought him here now? So to keep things real he reached for something business-like. "He was going to use the resin from the pines. He thought there was a big market for turpentine here."

To his surprise, Peter's expression changed to one of sympathetic curiosity. "From those pines, really?" Something had apparently caught his imagination.

Relieved now that he was not being thought mad, Levin pressed further into the hard realities. "It wasn't the best resin but good enough, according to Vincent. But the whole contraption was improvised and stuck together from odd parts, and the pressures were very high. I've wondered if it blew up or what."

"And that's why you came?" Peter asked, more intrigued than critical, which gave Levin the sense that maybe they shared some need, still undefined, or a view of some kind, a feeling. And with the relief of the confessor he laughed and said, "I wanted to find some way to get back up there, although it's probably gone by now. But maybe not."

"How do you plan to get up there?"

"I don't know. I thought I'd rent a car, if that's still possible. It's all pretty chaotic here, I understand."

"I'd take you up."

"Would you? That would be fantastic. I'm ready any time."

"How's tomorrow? I'll have to tend to some things around here first." Peter stood. Levin rose and offered his grateful hand, and feeling the power in Peter's grip, it seemed as if he'd crossed from water to land.

.   .   .

The Land Rover truck rode hard, its diesel engine sounding like a rolling barrel of bearings. Peter was wearing a tan shirt and white duck trousers, along with thick, well-worn work boots and a baseball cap with a Texaco logo. The sleeves of his shirt were neatly rolled up, exposing thick, tanned forearms as tight as the cheeks of a horse. Behind the front seat stretched a full-sized mattress covered with a red plaid blanket and two pillows at the forward end. The manager of the Gustafson, chatting with Levin at the hotel's entrance, had grinned on seeing this vehicle pulling up, and smiling wickedly, had said something about there having "been a lot of living on that mattress." And Peter was handsome with his clean, tanned face. He seemed eager, less guarded than on their meeting yesterday. As they left the city behind and climbed toward the pine forest he sounded happy, as if he welcomed the outing. "I haven't been up here since I was a kid," he said.

"Is there another road going up?"

"No. Why?"

"It doesn't look like I remember it. Wasn't there forest here?"

"Probably."

Peter had shifted out of fourth to third to make the climb and in places had to go down to second. On both sides of the road, bare soil dissolving to dust and sand stretched away into the distance. Levin's memory still held the image of the trees. Before them lay a beige-white expanse of bedrock where the pavement vanished.

"How far is it to the top?"

"At least an hour, maybe more on this road."

"Vincent had said they were stealing the forest."

"Yes, everything," Peter said.

"I can't believe this." Levin waved at the blasted landscape.

Peter merely nodded. It was hard to tell what he was feeling. He braked to a halt, estimating a gulley a couple of feet deep that cut across the road. Then proceeded into it and climbed back out, the truck's stiff frame groaning.

"Jesus, I remember a good road here."

"Erosion. With all the trees gone the last hurricanes really wiped things out."

"Looks lost forever."

Peter nodded slightly.

"It's like they ate the country and shat it out."

Peter glanced at him, and Levin regretted his outburst; things were so far gone here that indignation had to border on self-indulgence.

In fact, Levin's indignation reminded Peter of people he had known as a boy. His father and then grandma and his mother used to sound like this, like there was something to be done about things. The idea interested him, like old-time jazz, distantly. He liked the beat but the words were silly and ancient.

The bedrock was tilted here. Peter had to hold on to the door handle to keep from falling on Levin, who gripped the dashboard. Levin remembered nothing like this. Now, off to the right, there were people and what looked like tables set out on the ground. Peter headed across the rocky desert and stopped the truck. There were shanties clustered beyond the tables, a small village. The scene seemed as novel to Peter as to himself, Levin thought.

They were mostly women in rags, each hovering around her own table on which she had set out her wares, incongruous out here beyond any buyers. Peter and Levin moved among the tables, nodding to the women who barely acknowledged their greetings. On the tables were old combs, mismatched table-ware, knives and spoons and forks—some of them rusted—and on one table old pop bottles made opaque by sun and rain, bottle caps, pencils and pencil stubs, worn-out shoes, and every-where hunger-bloated children underfoot, some of them under a year old, mouthing dust. Peter picked up a small spoon engraved with unreadable writing and gave the woman money. Finally they came to a halt, looking around. People pretended not to be looking at them.

"Why do they do this, where would customers come from?"

Peter shrugged, and seemed annoyed by the question, as though Levin had spoken too loudly at a graveside. They went back to the truck.

The semblance of road was indicated by a few feet of snipped-off restraining cable that had once marked its edges. "Am I wrong?" Levin asked. "This *was* all forest, wasn't it?"

"I don't know. Probably. But the island had eighty percent of its surface in forest a hundred years ago, and it's less than three percent now." After a moment he said, "You say you met this Douglas guy?"

"Yes. Just briefly. I was only up here one day."

"What was he up to?"

"It's hard to describe. He was almost in a fever. Vincent thought he was slightly cracked, but that he wanted to do something for the country as well as for himself. Start a little industry and create some jobs, give the people some dignity. I heard him say that."

"Is that why you're interested?" There was no ironical inflection, no mockery in Peter's voice.

"I'm not sure," Levin said. "In a sense, I suppose, yes."

"In what sense?"

"I'm not sure how to put it exactly. I guess it was his conviction. It impressed me. In his crazy way I think he loved this place."

Peter turned abruptly to Levin, then back to the road. "What'd he love about it?" he asked. The question seemed important to him.

"Well, I don't know," Levin laughed, "now that you ask." After a moment he said, "You never heard of Douglas at all?" The truck was pitching wildly from side to side.

"No. But I was running around all over the place in those days, didn't stop to listen much." After a moment he asked rather shyly, "You came all the way down here for this?"

Levin was embarrassed. "Well, I don't have much to do. My wife is gone, practically all my friends. I'm not sure why, but the guy keeps coming back to me. I think about him a lot. And frankly," he tried to chuckle, "sometimes it seems like something I dreamed. And now, I come down here," he did laugh now, "and there are no witnesses left!"

Peter drove in silence, edging cautiously around the big holes. They'd begun to pass patches of surviving pines and the air had cooled. Levin continued, "To be perfectly frank about it, I really don't know why I came down. Except that I felt I had to. It's almost a question of," he laughed again, "sanity."

Peter glanced at him.

"I'd really like to find that still, if it's possible. Just to see it again."

"I understand," Peter said. And then he added, "I'd like to see it too."

They were grinding up out of a draw, and reaching the top, they saw a hundred yards ahead another Land Rover parked on the wasteland with half a dozen people seated around it. Peter pulled up and got out, and Levin followed him over to the vehicle, a taxi, which was listing sharply to the right. A man was lying underneath it—the driver, Levin gathered, trying to make a repair. The onlookers were an odd collection: a somber young woman in a short red dress with black net stockings and high heels and large brass earrings and hair piled high on her head was sitting on a newspaper on the dry ground; and beside her sat a short, large-bellied man with a pistol on his hip who occasionally eyed her like a dog guarding a sheep. A skeletal woman sat on a flat stone clutching a baby, and two others, a pair of young peasants, stood smoking, while another young man sat with his head between his knees.

No one spoke as Peter bent to see under the chassis. He had not greeted the people or taken any notice of them. Now he spoke Creole to the taxi driver, who ceased working and replied in soft tones to Peter's questions. Levin heard a clattering at his back and turned to see a brown, white-faced horse and rider galloping across the waste toward him. The horse was small but beautifully formed with an Arab head and slender, nervous legs which, when he was pulled up by the rider, never went still, its hooves constantly clacking against loose stones. Around the horse's neck a rope as thick as a hawser was neatly wound up to its jaws. The rider had long dreadlocks and a perky smile. "God's blessing on you all!" he called cheerfully. "Think of the sufferings of this world and thank your heaven for health and good spirits! I greet you, brothers and sisters, with all the good will in the creation!"

The group had turned to listen to him without reacting. Peter stood and walked up close to the rider and said, "They have a problem."

"Yes, I see," said the rider, "but we must have no doubt it could be much worse."

"I would like to buy the rope." Peter pointed at the rope wound around the horse's neck.

"Oh, I regret that is impossible. I need to tie him or he will run off when I get down."

"I would pay and you could find another rope."

"But how then could I get down?"

"You might find someone to hold him while you buy the rope."

"No-no."

"I will pay you a dollar American for the rope."

"No-no."

"Then two dollars."

"For this rope?" He seemed to be reconsidering.

"Yes."

"No-no," the rider said. The horse, its eyes rolling, suddenly danced a complete circle and faced Peter again. Unaccountably, the rider unknotted the rope, unwound it and let it fall into Peter's hand. Peter reached back for his wallet, but the rider, fighting to hold the reins and having to turn himself left and right to keep facing Peter and the group, lifted one arm and called out, "Remember God!" then crouched low to keep his seat as the horse flew off, its hooves sending loose stones clattering down the bare slope.

The unexpected gift of the battery thirty years ago crossed Levin's mind, and his back chilled. Peter crouched beside the truck and instructed the driver on where to place the jack under the frame. A U-bolt had broken, releasing the spring from the frame link. His commands seemed brutally brief, impatient, sometimes scornful. "No! To the left, the left, don't you know left from right? Hold it in place and pump it up. Good. Now come out." The driver squirmed out from under the truck, and Peter lay on the ground and slid in with the rope. The group watched without commenting, interested but keeping clear. Everyone waited in silence while Peter worked. Presently he slid out from under the vehicle and accepted with a nod—not quite of thanks but mute acknowledgment—a large blue bandanna from the man with the pistol with which to wipe his hands. The driver, exhausted, bone-thin, stood before Peter saluting.

Peter said, "Go slow. It won't hold very long. Very slow."

The group filed into the Land Rover. Levin brushed soil off the back of Peter's shirt. The man with the pistol shepherded the woman in the red dress, his hand hovering around her lower back. The man kept nodding obsequiously to Peter, who returned him his kerchief and gestured toward the revolver on his hip.

"You need that here?"

"The bad types are starting to come down out of the trees," the man said.

"No army up here? *Gendarmerie?*"

The man threw his head back with a silent laugh, saluted, and got into the Land Rover behind his woman.

Peter said nothing as he drove on, seemed angry. Levin felt responsible for his dirtied shirt, for the threatening pointlessness of the trip itself, even for the ugliness of the wasteland through which they had to pass.

"Strange thing, his giving you that rope for free," he said, trying to cheer Peter up. He then told him about the man lending the battery thirty years ago in very nearly this same place.

"What about it?" Peter asked.

"I don't know, it just seems unusual. Or do they normally help out strangers that way?"

Peter thought for a moment. "I don't think so. But I don't understand what gets into people anyway. I guess he just wanted to do it."

It occurred to Levin that Peter had stopped to repair the taxi with no thought of any kind of reward for himself. He felt ashamed, then stupid as he struggled and failed to understand the man beside him, just as he couldn't understand the horseman's gift, or the truck driver's so many years ago. Maybe what was so bewildering was Peter's lack of any sentimentality or enthusiasm about the people he was helping. There had even been a tone close to contempt in the way he'd ordered the driver around. Why had he bothered?

Scraggly pines were appearing now on both sides of the road, with numerous stumps between the trees. The road was black-top again here. Peter glanced at Levin and said, "We should be getting closer. You recognize any of this?"

"They lived in a bungalow off a side road. It wasn't far from the manager's office, if I recall. It came in from the right, I think, but it's hard to recognize it with the trees gone."

"I think the office would be a bit further up ahead, maybe we could ask there." But suddenly Levin recognized a pile of white stones beside a dirt road leading off to the right. "Here!" he cried, and Peter swerved the truck into the narrow road. And there, a hundred yards in, stood the bungalow.

Levin said, "Last time I saw this was thirty-three years ago." Peter pulled up before the porch. The screen was ripped and the door hung open, windows were broken, the place looked sullen. Levin got out and went onto the hollow-sounding porch, Peter behind him, and paused to look around at the junk still in the yard, the weeds, the dead bushes. He hadn't dreamed it, af-ter all; he could see Douglas scanning his blueprints and yelling for tea, and his wife appearing in her pink blouse and sling. They were going to beat the system, cruise the sea showing movies, lie on deck at night licking the stars. Then turpentine, be useful to the people, trying to *matter*. He walked into the liv-ing room. The four disintegrating books were still on the man-telpiece, and two long-cold carbonized logs lay half-burnt in the fireplace. The organ still stood against the wall. Douglas's wife had once invited him to play; now he would never learn how she'd known he could. He went to the organ. His steps seemed to echo. The ivory had been picked off the keys. He sat on a box and pumped, but the rotted bellows wheezed. He remembered her coming out in her pink blouse, her hand held protectively over the cast. He looked around. The room was as he remembered; there was nothing here to steal, and their dream and their wonderings were vanished with them. To be useful, he supposed, was the idea that had captured them and Vincent as well, but something else had won out in the end.

"I have a feeling I could find the still. We drove to it from here that day," Levin said as they walked outside. Peter seemed softened; "Was it like this before?" he asked. The romance of the search seemed to have entered him, and he liked it; Levin judged that it might be the profitlessness of it all that appealed to him, the romantic's natural attraction to lost things. Perhaps, Levin speculated, because his mother had chosen a new man to replace his father. Like Levin himself, Peter seemed to live with one foot over the edge searching for the cloud he could stand on.

Peter drove the truck onto the paved road and proceeded slowly, Levin watching the roadside tangles of vines and bushes for a sign. Peter slowed as they passed the manager's Alpine office, but there was no car parked in front, probably nobody inside. "Anyway, I'd rather not get the government involved," Levin said. Not since she died had he felt Adele's absence like this. He wanted her now, in the truck, saw her as she'd looked in her twenties, forty years before her death, with her flesh firm and her full arms around him. *I guess I'm also looking for what was lost,* he thought, and the idea seemed to illuminate his return to this place. It made him smile—*then it's her I'm looking for?*—he almost said aloud, and then he thought, *well, it's as good a reason as any.*

They continued on for a half mile. When Levin said he didn't recall the still having been this far from the office, they stopped and instantly heard a chain saw starting up nearby. They got out and found a narrow footpath into the brush, and after a short walk, came on four men hacking at a fallen pine, with a pile of stems nearby in a clearing. On seeing the strangers the men immediately stopped, waiting for the *blancs* to speak. They were all young, in their twenties, except for a bent, old, silver-haired man in a ragged overcoat, with a machete hanging from one hand and a stick for a cane in the other. He was catching his breath. Toward him Peter walked, and after a touch to his cap and a rather formal, quiet greeting, he asked him if he had worked around the area very long. The man said he had, all his life. The other men watched, alert as trespassers.

"There was once a *blanc* living over there in that bungalow with his wife and two children, he operated a machine to make turpentine. Did you ever hear of him?"

"I worked for him," the old man said, "when I was young."

"And is the machinery still to be found?"

"It's that way," the old man said, and pointed in the direction Peter and Levin had come from.

With the old man, whose name was Octavus, sitting between them they drove back along the paved road. He held the machete point down between his legs. He had tiny eyes in a flattened face, and his dank old man's smell filled the cab. "He smells like old iron, if that could smell," Peter said toward

Levin. Then to Octavus he asked in Creole, "Papa, are we getting closer or further away?"

"*Près, près,*" the old man said, pointing ahead.

"*Près* could mean a couple of miles," Peter said. Just then the old man jabbed his finger toward the brush, croaking, "*V'la, v'la,*" and laughing like they'd been playing a game.

Stiff as he was, Octavus had to slide himself across the seat and onto the ground like a board. Peter grasped his elbow as he moved unsteadily into the brush, parting it with his machete and straightening up to shield his face. He walks like he's parting the sea, Levin thought. The spiky vines snatched at their shirts and trousers as if defending a space. Levin, coming up behind, felt short of breath and recalled the altitude here, or was this his long-awaited heart attack? His slight struggling for air reminded him of Jimmy P.'s broken nose and how he would snort like a boxer whenever he exerted, the image reminding him that Jimmy must be dead some twenty-five years. And what happened to Jimmy's abject faith in the Russians, in the built-in virtue of the working class and the inevitable unspooling of history into benevolent socialism? Belief that profound almost deserved having dimension and weight enough to be buried; a national holiday might be good, perhaps, when people could visit their dead convictions. Funny, how it was easier to accept Jimmy's disappearance from the earth than that of his passion and all the mix of love and vengeance that had gone into it. What was more dispiriting than the waste of devotion that leaves behind the vanishing footsteps of the people it has misled? Or was there some other point to all the striving, he wondered.

They stepped into a clearing filled with stumps and weeds.

The old man stopped with Peter still touching his elbow, prepared to catch him if he toppled, and he pointed to the right, to a low butte with a dense mass of spiky vines at its base. The three men approached and peered through the vines, and once their eyes had adjusted to the dimness of the thicket, they saw deep within it a tall dark object, a black tube some six feet wide and maybe fifteen feet high. The thing leaned at an angle with its head raised against the butte as though it were resting, exhausted.

"I'll be damned," Peter whispered, "he really did it." And then laughed at its outrageousness, but his eyes were serious.

"Amazing, isn't it?" Levin said, glad now that Peter had found some excitement to make up for the troubles on the trip, and relieved also that the thing had turned out to be real. "He dragged it all the way up from the port!" He laughed, and in his happiness he couldn't help confessing to Peter, "You know, I was getting to where I wasn't sure I'd dreamed the whole thing, like I'd invented an obsession of some sort. I'm really relieved, though I still don't understand it."

"Well, you'd have to see it to believe it. I gotta get a closer look," Peter said, and he borrowed Octavus's machete and attacked the tank's vine barrier. Levin helped, dragging away the cut vines. "It's like a leopard's hideaway," he said, breathing hard. "We saw one once in Africa, my wife and I. Leopards are very secretive, live in the middle of thorn bushes, a lot like this." When they pulled away a dense eucalyptus the main tank was bared to the sunlight with a phalanx of smaller tanks piped together. Some pipes that must have connected to other tanks were amputated and ended in midair. The whole apparatus stood

over them like a snake-armed god, Levin thought, a presence, a
mute intention asking to be read. And it was much grander than
it had seemed at first, maybe twenty feet tall by eight or ten wide.

"Christ!" Peter exhaled, "he really *meant* it, dragging all this
up here!"

"I'd love to know if he ever lit it," Levin said.

Peter turned to Octavus and asked in Creole whether they
had ever operated the still. The old man sighed and lowered
himself onto a stump. Peter sat on the ground in an easy descent and translated as he spoke. Levin bent in a crouch and
tumbled back onto the ground. The old man's voice was hoarse
and cracked.

Mister Douglas had lit the fire and Octavus and three others
had milked the pines, and he recalled Vincent the Jamaican
who had supervised the process for only one day and then
never came back. They had made turpentine, which was like a
miracle coming from the pines, and everyone was given a liter
to keep from the first draw, and barrels of it were trucked down
to the port. And then sick people had begun showing up but
they had nothing to pay for turpentine so Mister Douglas would
give a cup or two to some of them for their bowels and skin
troubles and mouth sores and the babies until in the end there
were crowds of people some days, hoping for a cure of their
sicknesses. Douglas would even examine them like a doctor,
and his wife was like a nurse. "Some people paid with bits of
goat meat or garden beans, but he needed more money to oper-
ate, as I understood," Octavus said, "because my family has always run a store and I know about business. So Mister Douglas
went down to the bank at the port and they sent people up to

look at the thing, but they said it was not the right kind of pine and they wouldn't give him anything."

"We worked like this for five or six months," Octavus went on, "until one morning when we started to work he came and told us to stop and said he had no more money to pay us. We all sat down and talked about this but there was nothing anybody could think of doing, and so we went away and never came back. But my place is near so every few days I would stop by just to look around and see if maybe he was going to start up again, and one morning I found him bent over on the ground before the main tank like he was at prayer, but he was not moving and I touched him and he looked up at me, his face was only bone. His wife, I should mention, her arm had swelled up and she went back to the States for an operation and took the children and we never saw her again. But Douglas held my hand and we sat together on the ground for a long time. He spoke very good Creole so I remember it well. He said that he was dying now and thanked me for my work—I never allowed slacking on the job, and I was the responsible one over the others, you see. And he said that I should be the owner now, and handed me a paper from his shirt pocket which I couldn't read as it was in English. But the priest could read it and it said that I was the man inheriting. But where would I get the money to pay the workers? And so it ended."

"Was that the last you saw of him?" Peter asked.

"No, after a while I went to his house to see how he was faring now that I knew how sick he was, and he was alone there with one of the old women giving him goat's milk and so forth. He was glad to see me again and held my hand and then he wrote some words on a paper and gave it to me. I always keep it as I never saw him alive again."

He reached under his arm to a worn kid sack and brought out a yellowed patch of note paper with Douglas's name elegantly engraved on the top. Peter read it and handed it to Levin. *If the idea goes let it go, but if you can keep it, do so and it will surely lift you up one day.* It was signed, *Douglas Brown.*

Peter watched the old man intensely and now asked, "What idea did he mean?" Levin caught the tone of longing in Peter's voice.

The old man's head was square as a block; at one time he must have been very strong. He shook his head gravely and said, "I don't know. I never understood. The tanks . . ."

He broke off, turning to the tanks, staring at them for a long time, trying, it seemed, to bring something to the surface. Levin thought it must all seem like a dream to him too after so many years. The old man seemed on the verge of speaking but gave up, shaking his head, his small eyes blinking, and Levin thought, *And now it will all slide into oblivion, all that life and all that caring, and all that hope, as incoherent as it was.*

As they made their way out to the road, Levin saw a shiny bolt lying in the weeds. He picked it up and put it in his pocket, wondering what metal could have kept its shine after so many years. Levin, once inside the truck, saw that the old man was moved and looked satisfied. "He looks happier now," he said.

"Well, he passed it on," Peter said.

Swaying and thudding on its unforgiving springs, the Land Rover shouldered down the devastated mountain, the diesel grinding against the crazy tilts of the all but vanished roadbed. Staring out the window, Levin said, "They really destroyed the whole landscape. I would never have believed it was possible. And there was a pretty good road up here, you know."

Peter merely nodded. His silences, Levin understood now, were a kind of mourning for something far greater than his own life; the whole country was a surround of suffocating greed, inexpressible in the face of his hopelessness about changing anything. In the silence between them, Levin remembered once again how the last descent so long ago had brought him back with Vincent, dead Vincent now, to Mrs. Pat's house and to Adele to whom he had told the whole adventure that evening, and even how they had rediscovered their bodies that night in the broad beams of moonlight flowing into the room at the hotel, and it was once again inconceivable that she was no more, not to be found anywhere. They were two giants in bed, four feet sticking out from under the covers. How he had loved to *rely* on her body, feeling small sometimes on top of her. All gone. Pitching back and forth now between the unlined truck door and Peter's shoulder, the remorselessness of his loneliness astonished him. Douglas, he saw, had been driven crazy by hope. Hope on this mountain which even then, thirty years back, was being stripped of its life down to dead stone. Who could feel the quality of that hope anymore? Or was it illusion? But what was not? Up here he had caught a whiff of it again; blundering Douglas may have touched something almost sacred, having wanted to make a Madison Avenue life mean something and not knowing how except to do something so absurd. *And maybe that was why his image, after so short a time in his presence, stayed on in my mind,* Levin thought. It seemed now it would never leave him, even if he could only partially grasp its connection to himself.

He turned to Peter, whom, after all, he had known since he was a boy stuffing his mouth with cherries. "What do you make of it, Peter?" he asked.

"Make of what?"

"All this," Levin said, gesturing out the window. "Everything."

"Did you know my mother in New York?"

"Your mother? No, we met here. Why?"

Peter shrugged, but decided to continue. "They all thought they had the answer here. The political answer. Did you think that way?"

"Me? You mean some kind of socialism."

"Yes."

"I did, for a while."

"What happened to all that?"

"Well, the Russians, for one thing. The camps and the backwardness and so on soured people on it. And American prosperity."

"So it's all gone."

"Seems so, yes."

They rode in silence for a while. Here and there a lone man could be seen standing in the open, staring in surprise at them going by, his face dust-covered. "It's the end here, you know," Peter said.

Levin heard the depth of the loss in him, even though Peter's tone was dry and controlled. "You think you'll be staying on here indefinitely or . . . ?" He broke off, realizing that

Peter must love this country, and why prick at the pain of leaving it?

"I might go to the States, but I don't really know. My girl
wants to get married, but I just don't know."

"I'm curious, Peter—what are you feelings about Douglas?"

"I don't know. He was a damned fool, I guess."

"Because?"

"Well, he could have checked out the kind of pine he had
here before he got that far into it. And Christ, not getting his
technical information beforehand. That was stupid." He thought
for a moment. "But you'd have a hard time working with these
people no matter what you did."

"Why, what's wrong with them?"

"Their heads are someplace else. They see things we don't.
Hear things we can't."

"You have Haitian friends?"

"Oh sure, I was raised here. But most of them just fuck up
sooner or later."

"But they seem to have a sweetness," Levin said, thinking of
Octavus.

"Oh yes. Some." Then after a moment, "There's some very
bad people around now, and they're armed. With CIA help,
they say. Killings all the time."

"What will you do?"

"I doubt they'll bother me. If they did, probably because
they'd want a cut of my business. I'd have to close down and
get out if it's too much."

They were passing the small huddled shacks, the tiny gardens again. Levin turned the question over in his mind for a

few minutes, and finally said, "I thought the way you got that taxi going again was pretty terrific, Peter."

"I just tied the spring back on, that's all."

"I have to admit I was surprised you stopped and did that for them."

Peter seemed not to like where this was going and frowned. "I knew that guy."

"The driver?"

"Uh-huh."

"You didn't seem to from the way you talked."

"He's stupid. He shouldn't even be driving. He'd never have got that car going, didn't even know where to place the jack. He was trying to raise the car up instead of the spring, exactly the opposite of what he should have been doing. He's an idiot. Worked for me for a while till I had to can him."

"I see," Levin said. Then Peter had not been moved so much by some disinterested compassion or some knightly noblesse as by a kind of elegant impatience with the stupid driver and a pride in his own ability to make the repair? So the rescue was not as noble an act as he had imagined? Unless knights too had egos to massage. All Levin knew for sure was that he himself would probably not have stopped even if he'd known how to fix the taxi spring. Was it because he lacked Peter's love for these people? Or did he lack the wish to be anyone's seigneur?

He grinned to himself, thinking, *But if there'd been a piano out there on that waste I think I'd have been happy to sit and play for them while that driver bungled around and the people died of hunger and thirst waiting for someone to show up and save them. Chacun à son ego.* But then he thought again of the still, the size of the great main tank and the labor it must have taken to drag it up from the port and through the forest, plus the welder and his generator, and then of Douglas's frantic appeal to Vincent, his cracked and dirty eyeglasses crooked on his nose, and his outcry, "This country is *dying*, Vincent!"

Peter left him off at the hotel saying he would come by to pick him up for dinner that evening, clearly pleased to have new company. Levin waved goodbye and went up to his room. After a shower he lay naked on the bed, perhaps the same one he had shared with Adele. A car horn drifted through the shutters, which he recalled Adele had admired, and then a voice on the street in the chirping baby-talk language, then a roaring motorbike. He thought again of the tank and how it still looked in good condition, only a little rust along the welds. It could probably last a thousand years out there. In some sense it was like a kind of work of art that transcended the pettiness of its maker, even his egotism and foolishness. He felt glad he had come back here. Not that it meant anything, but he had inadvertently paid some kind of homage to Douglas's aspiration, an idea that he felt now had gone from the world, at least the world he knew. He loved Douglas and wished he could have been as careless with himself. He longed to play Schubert with Adele. He was falling asleep. There might be a piano in the hotel which he could imagine sharing with her beside him, he must ask the clerk. He could smell her scent. Odd, that she would never see the tank.

PRESENCE

He wakes at quarter to six, sun in his face, still tight about being criticized for not doing enough for women, slips into walking shorts and sandals with a glance toward her exposed arm, and thirsty for the morning fog steps out into the chill, walks toward the beach road in the swirling mist, grateful even to the dimmed sun for its uncomplicated touch of warmth on his back. The row of sleeping beachfront houses and their dozing cars alongside the road, his sandals whispering, he searches for the public path down to the beach and at last finds it alongside the last house in the row. On the brow of the path before it descends he pauses for his first glimpse of the sterling ocean, his hallowed homewater from so long past in childhood, when it loved him and scared him into sparkling and foamy white on top and dark below with live things in its holy depths. Once he had nearly drowned, at six, seven. Another step now descending upon the tippy, blanched gray planks, and through the long spear grass alongside him a white body suddenly, a man in his black T-shirt seen from his overhead vantage, fucking. He halts to watch. Slowly back and forth, a young body, tight and tanned, on his knees in hard control, but the crouched

woman all but hidden behind a hummock of sand and grass.
Without deciding to he finds himself turning back up the path
and halts witless beside the road. There is no other way to the
beach, he will have to wait. He parades in his loose sandals past
the beach houses not really too surprised that he is not aroused
himself. Possibly because there is something mute and controlled and therefore remote about this lovemaking, or maybe
it is his own repression. Whatever, it merely leaves him with
the restraint of courtesy. Which is soon superseded by resent-
ment at being barred from entering the beach; what an idea, to
do it ten feet from the public pathway! On the other hand, they
couldn't have expected anyone to come by at this hour. Still,
though, a few people must. Sure they must be finished, he re-
turns to the path and starts down again, managing to utter a
warning cough, certain they must be lying side by side this
time, probably covered by a blanket. At the dune's brow he
halts, seeing the man below him still fucking but a little faster
now, absolutely demanding, dominating, a Pan fucking earth
itself for all one could tell. A feather of something like fear now
at the sight, something sanctified in such power, the primordial
exchange of domination for submission. The man was now
lunging in quicker and longer and silently controlled strokes.
He turned, his mind confused, and walked back toward the
road before impending outcry, fearful of it now, not wishing to
witness its absurdly sacred thunder, as though in watching it
he would make it obscene, perhaps, or some challenge was
there he would rather decline.

Another stroll, longer this time, nearly the whole block to
the house where he and his wife were guests, and finally turn-

ing back in a last attempt to enter the beach, he mounted the
dune and descended. Fog had given way to pure Atlantic blue
sky. Beside the path lay the form of the man buried like a larva
inside a khaki sleeping bag, the woman gone. The ocean rolled
softly, at peace with itself, the scalloped spume washing the
gentle beige slope of packed sand. No one in the virgin water,
but now, off to the right, a woman in black shorts and a white
T-shirt, standing up to her ankles in the margins of the reced-
ing surf, bending over to thrash her open hands in the rest-
lessly churning suds. From his distance he could not tell what
she looked like excepting that her thighs were full and beautiful, but her hair seemed to stand up in stiff, wiry kinks. He
watched her staring out to sea, saw her climbing up the incline
and crossing to the soft sand. She saw him but did not let her
gaze linger and trudged back to their dune and spread out a
blanket and sat beside the hidden man curled up on his side. A
space of a foot or two separated them. She turned to look at the
pupa-like shape beside her. Then she looked at the sea again.
She wiped her hands dry on the blanket, then seemed to sigh
and lay down with her knees raised. After a few moments she
turned on her side, her back to the sleeping bag.

He walked to the edge of the sea, whose sibilant suck and
push had, he realized, been the sounds he had heard through it
all. Without a plan, he idled along the edge of the water away
from the pair. The sheer thoughtfulness of the ocean depths
stirred him; nothing in life was as dense with feeling, as wise
and deceitfully pleasing with its soothing strokes, while its
murderous temper was gathering hate. Breakfast hunger; starting back toward the path to the street, he was halted after a few

steps by the sight of them lying there some hundred feet away, the pupa shell and the woman curled up with her back to it, and he sat on the sand and stared. Why did he assume, he wondered, that she must feel deserted and unhappy now? Why could the guy not have been a stud with whom she wanted nothing more to do? Perhaps she had hunted him down, landed him, and now lay there the victor, resting before her next conquest. Mute as apes, he thought. Two of them in a cage with their silence and surfeit. And the sun. The sea's waves are the spin of the earth made visible. The young woman sat up, the man remaining inert in his shroud, having done what could be done with his earlier taunting of death. She was staring toward the sea, the length of beach still altogether empty. They must have slept the night there. It could have been their second fuck. She slowly turned now and looked across the light at him. He lowered his gaze deferentially, touched for some reason by guilt of his knowledge of her, then resolved to return her stare. She slid upward onto her feet and came walking over to him. As she approached, he saw the round of her hips and the bloom of her breasts. She was short. As she came closer he saw that her rigidly kinky hair had been only his illusion brought on somehow by mist and sunlight; she actually had heavy brown hair bobbed to the nape and round cheeks and dark-brown eyes. A widow's peak and orange coral earrings the size of half dollars. A Band-Aid around her left thumb; maybe she spent a lot of time on the beach with its broken bottles and splintery wood. She halted, standing over him where he sat cross-legged.

"Do you have the time?"

"No, but it's about half past six."

"Thanks."

She glanced full of indecision out at the sea behind him. "Do you have a house here?"

"No, I'm visiting for the weekend."

"Uh." She nodded deeply several times like a philosopher, but pretentious or not he began to feel she included him in her vision of things, whatever that was. She seemed to accept as inevitable his sitting there, the only one on the beach besides her lover and herself. She stood at her ease, pressing a loose edge of her bandage down on her skin. Then she turned from her thumb to him, her head tilted down to inspect him, take him in, a soft and slack smile broadening her mouth as though expecting some admission to come from him. He felt he was blushing. Then she sighed peacefully and looked once more out at the water, her uplifted chin lending her a certain nobility. He recognized the absurdity of his thought now that it was she who was in charge of the beach.

Something had happened. Uncomprehending, he realized with fear and unhappiness that he had made a link, was not alone, and resolved not to speak again unless to some purpose. Thirty years ago he had made love on this beach. There were fewer houses here then. It could have been in the grass on the same dune, although the one he remembered doing it on seemed higher. She was dead now, a skeleton by this time, he supposed. But they had not done it in absolute silence. And it had been in darkness, and he remembered the moon path shining on the water like a road, its light continuing into her black hair.

Was she not going to speak? He tried to seem amused but fear was mixed in him as he looked up at her. A quick glance told him that the sack had not moved, as though her partner had left for another world. But she was not sleepy. She might still be throbbing. Thoughts crossed the screen of her brow, her lowered eyes. From his angle her planted legs were like pillars rising from the sand.

"You watched us."

His breath caught but he clung to his right. "I had no idea you were there. . . ."

"I know, I saw you."

"Really? I didn't see you. You were hidden by the grass."

"I could see you, though. Did we look great?"

"Pretty great."

She turned and glanced toward the sack, shaking her head as though marveling at something. But letting herself down on the sand, she looked back over her shoulder again, apparently to make sure that he would not yet stir. Then she pulled her ankle under her thigh and sat almost facing him in a half-lotus position, her back straight. Now she seemed to have an almost Eastern visage, with her round cheeks pressing up her eyes into a narrowed gaze. "You came back once, didn't you?"

"Well, I thought you'd be finished."

"I couldn't actually see you, you know; but I felt you were there."

"How do you mean?"

"Some people have a presence."

Sitting in silence and staring at him, she seemed to be waiting for some agreed-upon thing to happen. He did not want to say or do something that might embarrass him or send him away. He turned out to the sea for a moment, pretending to relax with no necessity for them to speak because they were so secure in a shared silence. But she rose on oiled joints and walked yards into the water. He flushed with the beginnings of shame at losing her, then decided to follow and walked into the water behind her despite recalling the fine penknife in his pocket, his wife's birthday gift, which would be ruined by salt water. She slipped under a soft wave. The water was repellently cold, but he let himself into it and swam beside her. They treaded water facing each other, then she floated closer to him and laid a hand on his shoulder. He drew her in by the waist and then felt her legs opening and forking him. A wave lapped over their heads and they coughed and laughed, and she grasped his hips and pulled him to her and kissed him, her lips cold, then she slipped off and swam away and walked out of the water onto the beach, continuing up toward her lover who had still not moved.

Emerging, he reached into his pocket and drew out the penknife and opened the four blades, wiping them with his damp fingers and blowing moisture out of its nested interior, then sat on the sand. He had no towel but the sun was warming up. The fresh air in his lungs made him light-headed, and he threw his head back with his eyes closed to absorb everything in relaxation. There must be something he should do. He turned and looked up across the beach and found her staring at him where she sat on the blanket, and they held the stare like two ends of a long silken thread. Now he would lose her. Familiar aches were returning to his hips. Stretching out, he lay on his back with his small victory at having touched her body and somehow her spirit, and closed his eyes. Surprisingly, sleep's fingers began to creep into the backs of his closed eyes; a swim in the sea sometimes left him as relaxed as after sex, and he felt he could doze off now if he wished. A dreamscape began to form but the sun was rapidly heating up and would burn him, so he sat up and, starting to his feet, he glanced once more across the beach toward her protective dune and his heart chilled. They had gone. The shock flew into his stomach, threatened vomit. How was it possible so quickly? They would have to have folded her blanket and the man's sleeping bag and packed away some other things lying around. He hurried over to the dune where they had been but there was nothing, and the sand here was too loose to retain footsteps. A lump of fear swelled in his chest and turned him in all directions, but there was only the sea and the empty beach. He hurried over to the slatted path, hoping to reach the street before they disappeared, then halted, seeing a white T-shirt suspended on points of spear grass. Reaching down he took it in his hands and felt a very slight body warmth in the cotton. Or had it been forgotten by previous lovers and was only warmed now by the heat of the sun? A fear of having stepped over some restraining edge into utter loss. But at the same dark moment, a tremendous joy was flowing into him that was no longer connected to anything. He climbed the path to the street and turned up the road toward the house where he was staying. How strange, he thought, that it mattered so little whether or not they were actually here if what he had seen had left him so happy?